THE
GRASSHOPPER'S
RUN

THE GRASSHOPPER'S RUN

SIDDHARTHA SARMA

BLOOMSBURY

LONDON BERLIN NEW YORK SYDNEY

Bloomsbury Publishing, London, Berlin, New York and Sydney

First published in Great Britain in May 2011 by Bloomsbury Publishing Plc
36 Soho Square, London, W1D 3QY

Copyright © Siddhartha Sarma 2011

The moral right of the author has been asserted

A CIP catalogue record of this book is available from the British Library

ISBN 978 1 4088 0940 2

MIX
Paper from
responsible sources
FSC® C018072

Printed in Great Britain by Clays Ltd, St Ives Plc, Bungay, Suffolk

1 3 5 7 9 10 8 6 4 2

www.bloomsbury.com

Putting the front sight on a sod hut and on a person are two different things.

Elmore Leonard, *Valdez is Coming*

These impulses had been uncommon lucky, but I couldn't go on like that for ever. *Ek sal 'n plan maak*, says the old Boer when he gets into trouble, and it was up to me now to make a plan.

John Buchan, *Greenmantle*

PROLOGUE

The village should not have been where it was, when it was, but these matters cannot be changed in a moment. So it was there, then, on that day. And all the events that happened afterwards happened.

It was not so much a village as an exclamation mark of little thatch huts, goat and pigpens running down the angular face of the hill. It was shut in on three sides by the nearer hills, which came down to the little stony stream at the base of the ravine.

The hill on which the village itself stood was surrounded by thick oak and alder in a wide radius, and was far away from any trail going west into the Naga Hills. It was the easternmost settlement of the tribe, just west of the Dikhow river. It was also considered by everyone who knew it as remote, protected and as safe as possible in times such as these.

The Colonel of the Imperial Japanese Army who crouched beneath an alder looking down over the crest of the hill at the village thought so too. Inaccessible. Cut off. The place could not be found even if someone took great care to look for it. In fact, he thought to himself, after he won this campaign, after Japan won the war and he became a celebrated veteran and lectured to officers at the new Senior Course Academy in Kanagawa, he would talk about camouflaging an operations base and how the British did it.

Which goes to show that he was not only an ambitious soldier and a tactical mind, but also a man who counted his poultry farm before the eggs arrived.

He was also harried. For nearly a week he had been playing hide-and-seek in these green hills and ravines, with his crack unit, parallel with elements of his division further south and west. He was tracking the British 50th Parachute Brigade's elements, one of the few hurdles to the invasion. That brigade was scattered somewhere around here. He did not have to seek them out; it was a job for—he thought —lesser men. He was more useful to his superiors as a planner than a fighter, but for this once, if he could find that irritating brigade, why not?

Various signs showed the village was not empty like the few they had passed on their march west. Tracks in the hills, freshly-cut wood. For the Japanese officer, these were means to cover up the British presence in this harmless-looking collection of huts. The livestock could be another deception.

His deputy now told him the men were in position. Three crews manning Type-3 heavy machine guns covered the village from different angles, their firing arcs converging at the approximate centre. The 250 men under his direct command would follow their *Rikugun Taisa* unquestioningly, as they had through the plains and mountains of China and the ravines of northern Burma to this.

He was certain the new arrangement would give him a chance to shine in the eyes of his superiors. The generals might disapprove of his methods sometimes, but here at the gates of India he would show them what he was.

There would be no warning, none of that translating garbage he had to pass on to his troops earlier. This was certainly the British brigade or a part of it, as he had radioed to his division. He ordered the attack.

For a moment, his mind considered the possibility that he could be wrong, and he should wait for confirmation. Just as quickly, he told himself it did not matter at all. If he was right, good. If he was wrong, it was only a waste of ammunition.

In fact, on that afternoon beneath that mildly sunny sky on that hill, the Colonel and his intelligence were both wrong. The British 50th Parachute Brigade under Brigadier Hope-Thompson was at that moment 120 miles to the south, near Imphal, and they too were tracking the enemy. Two days later, the British were to meet Major General Shigesaburo Miyazaki's 58th Regiment at a place called Sangshak, which they would hold over six days of close fighting, taking murderous losses until the defenders ran short of water, were outnumbered and withdrew.

But that was in the future, so now the Colonel watched as his troops drew their rifles, the machine gunners jacked their levers and the firing began. The lead heavy machine gunner, firing into the huts, drew a line roughly north-south, bisecting the village and those who ran out of the huts now. Unsurprisingly, these were older men, women and children, and as they came out they were cut down in the first salvo, screaming and flailing as the steady liquid *clack-clack* of the heavy Nambu machine guns gave a finality to the matter.

The Colonel saw the first few go down, waited to see if troops came out behind them. But there were only more of these local hill people, little better than the Ainu back home, those half-animals up on Ezo Island. How they and these lived, if at all they were human, was beyond his understanding. Anyway, he could not let them get away to tell the British. He ordered the men to keep firing. The men, always in awe and fear of their Colonel and the stories they had heard of him, obeyed, though not without hesitation, for these had been normal men when they had begun a little more than a year earlier.

It took ten minutes. The machine guns drove through the walls of the huts, drawing the people out, and the riflemen aimed and shot, aimed and shot. The last of the stragglers went down and the troops were ordered to sweep the village.

The soldiers walked softly downhill into the village while others set up a perimeter in case the enemy was sighted, some going down to the creek to check for the wounded. The others entered the huts, firing at the wounded or those who still moved, not acts of mercy but to finish the job. Far away a hornbill called, and the screams of the dying answered.

It is a miracle of sorts that he had survived the barrage, but maybe not a miracle, because the riflemen were firing at the running villagers and the machine guns were firing at the huts, but at waist-height. Whatever the reason, or maybe because he had kept his head, the boy had hidden in some corner somewhere.

Superior Private Kawabe stepped through the door of the wood-and-thatch hut and died, the foot-long throwing spear or *nu* impaling his throat to the mud wall. The second soldier brought his Type-38 rifle up and went down with another spear in the centre of his chest.

The Naga crossbow is not a weapon of war, because traditionally Naga engagements (sadly more often against opposing Naga tribes than invaders) have been close-range ambushes with knife, spear and machete. But the boy leaped out through the window behind the hut, landed on his feet effortlessly and shot the first rifleman running around the corner, the ten-inch iron-tipped and rooster-feathered arrow, meant for running boar at thirty feet, sticking through his heart and out behind his back.

The next Japanese did not have time to point his rifle as the boy, trying to take the quickest way out, was on him, his wood-handled knife stabbing, stabbing horizontally through his ribs, stabbing as they tumbled in each other's grips, stabbing and tearing at his clothes, stabbing until the others clubbed him on the head again and again.

When he came to, he was tied to a cattle stake, bloody and bruised. His head was bleeding where they had nearly broken it in, his ribs hurt where they had kicked him afterwards in rage. A group of Japanese was talking, explaining to what he thought was some kind of leader.

The boy was beyond being afraid now, even if he did not look around at what had happened to his people. Some part of his dazed mind told him what would happen to him, but the other parts were beyond caring. So these were the Japani.

From somewhere where such thoughts seem to stay, he remembered his mother now, when he was a little boy before he went to the *morung*. 'Uti, little Uti,' she was saying to him. And his brother. Always, little Uti and his friend together, and they knew she would tell them a story.

'Uti, shall I tell you about the Molomi?'

And that was the story they heard so many times, his brother and he. Each time she made it sound different, something new to hear in the same ancient story of the End of the World, the Fire from the East and the Water from the West. And always, always, the Grasshopper.

He smiled a little now, looking at the Japani's dead eyes and remembering his mother's as she told them of the Grasshopper. And how the boys would talk about it later and how they would argue about if it was a true story, his brother scoffing at his belief.

Now at the cattle stake near the pigpen, Uti understood because he had always believed. So this was the Fire from the East. He understood and he remembered how the story ended.

You can burn me now, Fire, he thought, though he could not imagine what dying would be like. You can kill me.

The tall man, with the long knife at his belt, looked at him now and again, nodding at his men, reassuring. Such things happened, he seemed to be telling them.

6

The Colonel was, in truth, secretly amused. Plan for a brigade, he thought, and what you get is a half-animal with a knife.

'Ask him where the British ... no, of course you don't know what he speaks, do you?'

His adjutant shook his head.

'Hmm. All right. Finish him, but make sure he knows first what it means to kill the men of the Retsu Heidan.'

And that was that.

You can burn me now, Fire, thought the boy. You can burn everything you want.

The Grasshopper will come looking for you.

It took another half an hour. The screams, if any, were swallowed whole by the hills and the forest and the light breeze which came now.

The group of armed runners, racing in from the west with a message from an old man to leave the village quickly, arrived three hours too late.

It was the evening of 18 March 1944.

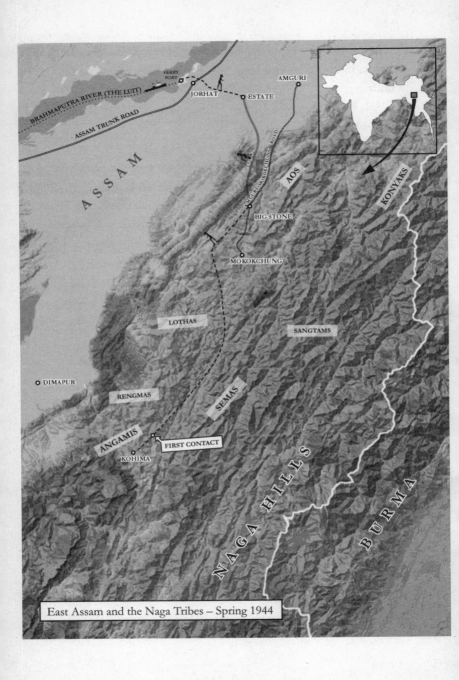

East Assam and the Naga Tribes – Spring 1944

1

The hall *khalasi* knocked on the door a full hour before time, discreetly but just loud enough. The boy came off the bed as he always did, almost fully awake. Some part of his mind told him instinctively it was too early for his wake-up call, and the blackwood Siemens on the wall confirmed this.

In most ways, the boy was a creature of routine, a routine he had created to make sure he did not become like, say, 'Hendy' Henderson, the other sleeper, whom nothing short of a Jap bomb could wake up before eight.

Gojen Rajkhowa, however, was a runner. He was many things, including the A team keeper, but of all things in this school, he was a runner. Each day he woke at dawn and ran five to seven miles, alternating with quarter-mile sprints every weekend, long easy strides across country, smelling the dawn and hearing the dawn sounds, pacing himself.

He was glad to study in Bengal, as close to home as possible then, but the earth did not feel the same. It had the smell of too many people living and cultivating the same patch over too many centuries, too much history of famine and misery, not like home, not like the feel of the fertile fields and the nearness of the forests and the hills and the rains.

He was on the big side for his age, had rather oversized hands; his bones were long and he was slim, even lanky, not too big or deeply insulated but tough in the way boys recognise quickly and learn to avoid. If you asked them why, they would not have given a plausible answer. It was an instinct, that was all.

His face, on a short but thick neck, was plain and unremarkable, even ordinary. People passed him by without a second glance. Which he liked. His cheekbones, seen in a certain light, were high, the mark of his Thai ancestors, but his eyes were not nearly as Mongoloid as other Ahoms'.

He was popular in his way, as a good keeper, and had a few friends, English, Scottish Protestants and a few Irishmen and Indians, had learnt their humour and handled his soup spoons and butter knives with the knowledge of fifteen years of careful breeding. They liked him for his ease and comfort among them, his friendliness, his family's background. He belonged, they all thought.

Sometimes he would walk the grounds or the fields outside and his eyes looked and saw everything, but differently: distances, heights, gradients, the position of the trees and their proximity to each other, the flight pattern of some bird.

And, more important, remembered.

He would often choose places from where the view was wide and far. He would sit and look at the distance, his body still, his hands and feet steady, not moving at all. His friends noticed his capacity for immobility, a complete inertness when he sat like this, but it was not stiffness either, nor was he uncomfortable. It was a type of ability.

He was also disgustingly good at mathematics, but this was no surprise to the one man in the school who knew who he really was.

'A man is here to see you, sir,' said the *khalasi*, with the proper respect kept for residents of the school and the masters.

Something in the way he said 'man' clicked in the boy's head, for he had an ear for these differences. Whoever it was, and the boy seldom had visitors, was unexpected and different to the bearer's experience.

The man was sitting in the shade of a mango tree, one of several on the new grounds of the school, which had shifted here outside Calcutta two years ago, after the city was bombed by Japanese aircraft. Some would call this a needless precaution, shifting an entire school for a distant war, but the parents were such that when they made a suggestion, it was usually followed.

The boy saw the man first and it touched him that he had shown the courtesy to wear a *dhuti-panjabi* as a gesture to the city he was in. It was as much an effort at blending in, at not drawing attention, although the man's face, his swarthiness, his build and the honour-tattoos peeping out from the collar at the neck said something else.

'Mopumeren, *khura*,' said the boy, smiling. Among them he addressed each by name but for this man he also said 'uncle'. 'If we get you a Gandhi cap you will look ready to join the protesters. Only way I can get thrown out of this school now,' he said, needling the older man. But he saw his particular type of humour was not much use.

'What brings you here? When did you arrive?'

'Shiluti is dead.'

Like that. There was no hesitation, no outward sign of grief, no method or formula for breaking the news. Mopumeren knew this boy could take it, like he could.

The boy sat down next to him and stared at nothing. Like that. Uti was dead. The words went around inside his head and he sat there for a long time and a short time.

'How?'

'Japani. Your grandfather heard they were moving into our hills in large numbers and he told the old man. We all knew the Japani were in Konyak land, but we never thought there were so many of them. The old man sent runners to all the villages there, but when they reached Uti's ancestral village they found the whole village killed.'

The whole village. Eighty people from Uti's tribe, in their ancient village. Secure in their belief that, as in the past, no one would come across the ravine. Underestimating the speed with which this invader moved and went everywhere. Not understanding that this was a different war.

'They tied him to a stake and cut him, I think with bayonets. I think they enjoyed it. They bled him a lot before he died.'

Gojen said nothing.

'The old man sent me to you by the first ferry. He wants ...'

'I am going back with you.'

'He said it depends on you. But he wants you to do something first.'

The man brought out a small parcel wrapped in palm leaves to keep it dry. 'The runners did not stay to bury the people but they brought Uti back and buried him at Mokokchung. Other people buried the villagers. But the runners found this behind a hut.'

The boy took the piece of paper from its wrapping. It was a better kind of mill-made rice-paper, but coarse still, the print smudged in parts. It was covered in what the boy thought must be Japanese, although he could read the English sentences.

'The old man wants to know who did this, boy. He wants to know who was there. He knows these matters as well as I do. The runners tracked about 200 men there. Someone

12

was leading them. I know of such raids. They fire first from a distance and check for survivors later. Uti must have hidden somewhere when they started firing and killed some of them when they came to check. This must have fallen out of the clothes of one of them. The old man says you study with the sons of big Ingraz, eat with them. Find out what it says.'

'Meren, you wait here.'

The boy knew who to ask.

*

The Reverend George S. Bartlett, MA (Lit. and Theo.), headmaster, a respected man of letters and also a man with something of a past, had sat down for breakfast on his lawn when Gojen walked up to his fence-gate, tieless but in his hall shirt and khaki shorts and let himself in.

Bartlett was in his mid-forties and had mild manners, although the junior classes were much in awe of him and more concerned that he was a good middle-weight who still sparred. Greying brown hair, hard brown eyes, the kind of eyes that seemed to have seen a whole lot more, and worse, than volumes of literature and theology. He was still in shape and would continue to be. He, too, was a creature of those habits which help when the time comes to cast them off.

'Ah, Rajkhowa, I was expecting to see you run past shortly. You may sit down, but if you plan to run afterwards you will stay away from the toast and marmalade.'

The boy sat down on one of the cane chairs. Between him and the headmaster was a special bond of a different nature, that of mutual respect, bordering, on the older man's side, on occasional amazement. The boy was always correct and formal in Bartlett's presence, even during his visits to

Gojen's father's plantation and their travels in the forests. But he also knew he need not hesitate with Bartlett.

Rajkhowa was a third-generation student here. His grandfather and grand-uncles, his father and all his uncles had been here, and he was the first of his generation. Although it was joked sometimes back home that all that education had not made them entirely sane, they were as much a tradition here as Evening Service and Family Visit Day and Matriculation results.

'Sir, you remember Shiluti?'

The headmaster nodded, his attention on the boy, knowing he had not dropped in (without a tie) for a mere hello. 'Yes, of course, Shiluti. Shilukaba's grandson. I remember. Remarkable boy. It's a pity we can't have him here as well, instead of living with the old man. He has the makings of a fine man.'

'He is dead.'

And the boy explained, as the Naga had to him. The headmaster took it as he had, grave and silent, dispensing with the usual solicitations, for he was a similar man. The boy gave him the paper.

'I thought maybe you could have a look at this and tell me what it means. The old man thinks it could tell us what happened.'

Or who it was, but he did not voice that.

Rev. Bartlett took out his spectacles and frowned over the paper, ignoring but not forgetting the brown smudges on it.

'It looks like a translation script, as I am sure you have guessed. We were given some of these during the war, you know. Who is your commander, put down your rifle, put your hands up, that kind of thing. Helps when you are fighting someone who doesn't talk your language. Same as the English sentences, probably some very basic words. I am afraid I don't know Japanese, my boy. But since it comes with a heading and is signed by someone or the other, I think … yes, we can find a name.'

The headmaster thought for a while. He, too, knew the right person to ask. 'Who brought the message, an Ao?'

'Yes, sir.'

'From the way they treat you, he must be a chief. Tell the *khalasi* to have the guest room ready, and tell the gentleman he is welcome to stay here.'

And meanwhile, I will get to the bottom of this.

*

Calcutta was under siege. From the middle of 1941, blink-and-you-miss-it Dum-Dum Airport and the smaller RAF strip at Barrackpore had been bursting at the seams with RAF and Royal Navy Aviation transports, fighters and bombers. The train station was filled with soldiers, the harbour and small jetties up and down the Hooghly blocked with uniforms and suppliers' consignments. From 1942, the Americans had joined the show. Civilian traffic—what few flights there had been before the war—was almost dead, commandeered aircraft too bringing troops and heavier transports flying in tanks and artillery, all heading north and east into Assam, Burma and beyond. Squadrons of fighters and bombers refuelled and flew east.

On 2 December 1942, the 1st Imperial Japanese Air Force squadrons had hammered the former Indian capital with bombing raids. Their target was Howrah Bridge, and although they missed that artery, they did succeed in bleeding the city of more than 250,000 civilians who decided life was too short to be given up between the British and the Japanese.

Calcutta was otherwise as it had always been, but since

15

1911 it had been settling into a kind of disgruntled decline, as if it had woken up one morning to discover 'What! I am not the capital any more?' and had refused to believe it since. It was a look and an architectural attitude that would last for a long time.

Opposite the faux-Minerva Temple Mint and two hundred yards down Strand Road, down a quiet alley, was a thick teak door. Just a plain unadorned door, with no markings or signs indicating what it might be, except a small insignia of some regiment or the other that hinted at an Army connection. The huge Pathan at the door was enough notice to the accidental visitor to stay away.

Rev. Bartlett was let in to the club or café, or a judicious cross of both. Inside were dark brown leather chairs and recliners and a few diners, none he recognised, a constant possibility in this place where the cream of the armed forces of the Raj sometimes gathered. His man, as he knew, was in the smoking section and had probably been drinking for a while.

'Why, bless me, 'tis the Reverend Private himself,' said the thickset man in civvies, rising and snapping off a salute and for added measure, a Catholic three-finger benediction.

'Kenneally, glad you could make it,' said the Reverend, settling down and pulling up his cuffs.

'Of course, I don't mind. I am at a loose end as always. Hardly anything to do,' said the other.

It was as much a lie as the Catholic salute. Lt Colonel John Kenneally, formerly of the Irish Guards Regiment, now a mover and very shaken shaker with the Intelligence Corps, was one of the busiest and most-cursed soldier boys in Calcutta at that moment.

Kenneally was an Irishman, but with many differences. For one, he was Protestant. For another, he had been born and lived in England throughout, son of a dock worker from Liverpool, where he had grown up and got a decent school education before joining the Guards' draft in 1914. One of the few Irishmen Bartlett knew who could not box, Kenneally had a dogged persistence while on a case, a quality appreciated in the Intelligence Corps if not in civilian intelligence, which demanded the flashes of brilliance of the Oxford dons who populated it during this war.

The waiter came and topped up Kenneally's whisky, good strong Army drink as always, but Bartlett, remembering he had to lead Evening Service in school that evening, chose a light port.

The two men went back a long way, longer than anyone would have guessed now, looking at the career soldier and the career cleric. Nearly two-and-half years in the trenches of France can create a bond not easily understood by those who never slept with French rats and German artillery shelling for company or jumped the barbed wire half in obedience to someone's orders, half to get away from the rats.

'You have been fine, I can see that. Takes more than war rations to remove the shine from young Bartlett's apple cheeks, I have told myself,' said Kenneally.

'The school is fine,' the Reverend acknowledged.

The drinks arrived.

'Well, what else, to Triumph and Disaster, the two Imposters,' said Kenneally, raising his whisky. In his cups he tended to overdo the club routine.

'I met him, you know, in 1934 in England,' said Bartlett.

'Who, Jack's father?'

'He was all right, it seemed. We talked about the War. I told him about how much that poem meant to us in the trenches. Suppose he heard that all the time.'

'He took it hard. Pity.'

'To Jack, and all the Jacks this show is throwing up.'

'To Jack. *Quis separabit.*' Who shall separate us: their regimental motto.

And the two soldiers drank to the third, and remembered a slight, bespectacled young man who had shared the trenches with them for a day at Loos in 1915, shared the brotherhood of all soldiers of all times but had never returned home.

'John, I have something here I want you to see. This remains between you and me, mind.'

The Lt Colonel became brisk and interested. 'Ah, business at last. Out with it.'

He took the piece of rice-paper and examined it. He didn't need spectacles. He took his time, which usually meant he was supremely interested.

'George, George,' he said at last, grinning like a cadet and waving the paper. 'Own up. What have you been up to? Where would an apparently respectable pillar of the C of E get *this*?' He was agitated.

'I cannot tell you that. Someone I know died and this was found near him.'

'Come on, I can see the dried blood as well you can. Where?'

'I cannot tell you that.'

'Where?'

Bartlett hesitated.

'Out east.'

'Where, Burma, Assam, bloody Singapore?'

'Near Burma.'

'That's Assam.'

'Somewhere near it. I cannot tell you more.'

Kenneally's eyes narrowed inquisitorially. 'George, don't tell me you are like what's-his-name, that fellow. You know, preaching by day and cloaking and daggering by night ...'

'I don't know, Thomas More? Of course not, don't be an idiot.'

Pause.

'This chap who died, one of ours?'

Of course, the real question. One of ours, one of theirs, one of God-knows-whose. Draw the lines, determine the damage.

No, Kenneally, loyal eavesdropper to His Majesty's Forces, thought Bartlett, don't get me into that.

'No.'

'So, a native. Let me see. Japs come across him, he puts up a fight, they snuff out his light.'

'Actually, it was an entire village.'

'Obviously, seeing from this. Tell me, you know any Japanese?'

'Not at all.'

'Hmm. I do. I know a damn sight more Japanese than I care to, anyhow. But you knew it, so you brought me this piece of paper.'

'You know what it says?'

'Of course I do. Now tell me why *you* want to know.'

'Academic curiousity.'

Kenneally snorted. 'You are no more an academic than I am a belly-dancer. You want to know what and why and, in particular, who was the beggar behind the show, that's what you want.'

It was too true to deny.

'I'll give you the short version for now, but let me tell you, old boy, this paper is a coup. For me. Yes, indeed.'

Go on.

Kenneally composed himself like an orator, for the vanities of youth die hard, and many ages ago he was the student and Bartlett was the shooter.

'This here is a translator's paper, like always. The Nips give it to a few in each unit, just in case they seem to be in the mood for prisoners, which they are not in Burma, by God.'

'How are things there?'

'You heard about Hope-Thompson?'

'All over the papers. The Brigade withdrew.'

'Didn't have a choice. Best he could do was a delaying action. The Japs are swarming into Assam now. We are sending men as fast as possible into those bleeding hills. Why, the brass plucked out a whole bunch from amphibian training down in Madras for some lunatic plan of landing on the beaches of Burma, and is rushing them by yesterday up the hills. Much good that will do. They want Kohima and Imphal and all points west. Beyond that, we don't know for certain. And if the boys here stopped protesting and wanting us out it could be easier. You didn't hear it from me. Now this … this paper. It upsets everything.'

I am still listening …

'At the top, see this? That's Hohei Sanju-ichi Shidan. IJA 31st Division. That's the lot up there. Next to that, typical Jap beggars, that's Retsu Heidan. Furious Division. That's their call sign. What they are furious about, I don't know. Bunch of second-raters, if you ask me. Set up Bangkok, 22 March last year. Reservists. Not good enough for the Pacific or the swamps out in Indonesia, but their top hats think good enough for India.' He was reciting from memory now, touching on a familiar obsession.

'This one is the 1st Communications Unit of the Division. Far as we know, set up as a backroom monitoring and reconnaissance unit. Special command structure. Last heard of forty miles east of the Chindwin. Seen near Tamu, small border town east of Manipur, maybe six weeks ago. Then, nothing.

'This document is so much wind, simple instructions for their Privates and Superior Privates. But it is signed …'

Here Kenneally leaned forward as much as his bulk and the table permitted, looking comically intense, staring at Bartlett.

'What do you know of Nanjing?'

And Bartlett chanced on something big.

On 13 December 1937, Nanjing, the capital of the new Chinese Republic was finally occupied by the Japanese. Almost from the moment the soldiers entered the city, till February the following year, civilians and prisoners of war were lined up and shot. For being soldiers, for being sympathisers, for simply walking past the occupiers, for the flimsiest of reasons.

'That is right. You know how many? Our government and Uncle Sam agree to 200,000, but I think it is more. It is always more, and you know this as well I do,' said Kenneally, draining his whisky and calling for more. He had a special dark place in his heart for massacres.

He had good reason to. On 3 May 1916, armed Irish Catholic militiamen had burnt his grandmother's farmstead at County Kildare with her, Kenneally's uncles, aunts and cousins inside. What made it worse was it was a planned tactic in a war of attrition where such attacks against civilians were secretly encouraged by both sides.

'Timperley, that was the *Manchester Guardian* chap in China, sent despatches through most of it. They did not print the worst of what he mentioned, obviously. I have copies of them all. Another fellow called Magee made a film or something. Things to give you nightmares, Bartlett. Nightmares. I have a cutting from a Jap newspaper. These two Jap soldiers with their swords, the headline talking about how they had a contest to see who killed more than a hundred fastest.'

Kenneally went on, remembering. Bartlett had heard some of it from him before, but this was a letting go. 'One of them, Mukai, I think, had 106. The other, Noda, had 105. Posing with their swords for the newspapers.'

He shook his head to snap out of it.

'Sorry, forgot myself there. Anyway, the Japs were commanded by Asaka, one of their princes. I suppose after the war when we line them all up they will go red shouting they only followed orders. Your man here,' he tapped the sheet, 'Colonel Shunroku Mori. As special advisor on the staff of General Iwane Matsui at Nanjing. Know who he is?'

'Mori? Never heard the name before.'

'The greatness of evil is in its anonymity, isn't it? Graduate from their Army War College, Tokyo, 1930 or thereabouts. Classmate and close friend of Hattori, who is now secretary to Prime Minister Tojo himself. Mori is right up there with the high rollers in Tokyo. Another junior from the same college, chap called Tsuji, planned the Singapore invasion and Pearl Harbor. Now, Mori was on that staff back in Nanjing, see? Made all the plans for the occupation. A typical backroom tactician : planning, plotting, hungry as old Bonaparte. Without a doubt he was the one who came up with the massacre idea.

'Mori went to Singapore in '42 and what do we have? Sook Ching. Same, what do you say, *modus operandi*. Catch 'em, kill 'em, yee-haw! Sorry, our American cousins' methods of expression seem to rub off constantly.

'Anyway, Sook Ching. Chinese and Malays. I honestly do not know how many. I don't want to know. Sods even have a word for it. They call it *Kakyoshukusei*. Purging the Chinese.'

'That's enough whisky, don't you think?'

'Nothing wrong with the whisky. Nothing wrong with me. Anyhow, there's your chap. He has personal and absolute command over this unit. Two massacres known,

22

this little one now, God knows how many from China to Burma. Stops at nothing, thick with the high rollers, *sake* mate with everyone except Hirohito, and that must not be through lack of trying, I'll wager. If I could get my hands on him, I could put up so much evidence to hang him a hundred times over. Didn't think I would get the chance.

'Now, you say he is somewhere in Assam commanding his personal bunch of recon beggars who think he is halfway there to Confucius or whoever they worship, and I tell you this. If he is here, the Japs have not come for bloody Kohima or for bloody Imphal. He won't even stop in Calcutta. That man is going straight to Delhi as surely as you shot that German at 150 yards, back in '15.

'So you tell your native boys or whoever gave you this to pack their hearths and homes on their outsize cows and run off the hills like the devil's right behind them. Because he is. Tell them old Kenneally said this, and he knows.'

2

Home. Or near enough, thought Rajkhowa. They were crossing where the Manas river met with the Brahmaputra or as he preferred to call it, Luit, and hundreds of years of being the western tip of the Ahom kingdom gave it the feel of crossing a certain line. Home. Or near enough.

The river here was broad and both banks were pushed far away near the horizon. To the left, southwards, was a hint of pale blue against the cloudy sky, the first of the Khasi and Garo Hills. Nearer and along the banks were the swamps. The river was a muddy mass of fast currents, undercurrents and small whirlpools. They would sometimes pass fishing boats and cross-bank ferries, fishermen with their nets cast into the waters for the good catches they would get just before the rains set in.

Occasionally he saw a grey shape break water, and he made a quick estimate of its speed, the ferry's speed, relative distance and time, looked ahead and at the exact spot he looked, the dolphin broke for air again.

This was a week into the journey upriver from Calcutta, and the boy was sitting in his favourite spot on these passages, up atop the steering cabin aft of the ferry, which from a distance looked more like a three-

24

storeyed house floating ponderously on the river than a steamboat.

Coal was not a problem in Assam, with its mines, and the ships, made of steel and floored with wood, had comfortable rooms for families for the ten days of travel from Calcutta to East, or Upper Assam.

The boy sat atop the cabin where a bearer would call him down for lunch, glad no one on the ship—filled more with soldiers than Assamese—had recognised him. He did not want anyone, except the unavoidables, to know he was coming home. Mopumeren was somewhere on the bridge, talking to some acquaintance he had made.

The boy was in his shorts, vest and barefoot. If the sun came out he would have to step down before the tin roof heated up, but for now the river breeze nudged his toes and round the side of his neck and the letter in his hand.

He opened the letter again. He remembered each word, but still.

Kenneally, protesting and cursing fearsomely that he was sober, had finally agreed to give a brief *curriculum vitae* of Mori to Bartlett. He also agreed to cough up, after due protest and claims that the Reverend was taking undue advantage for saving his life in France, a photograph.

'What purpose this will serve,' he had written and sent by special messenger the following day to the school, 'I do not know. I have informed the brass about what I think, and I put your paper on the file. Don't fret: I have only mentioned you as "an informant". That might start a few things, but I am not sure. The men up there will have more on their plates than to look for one Jap. I suppose if he is still alive after the war I can have a go at him. Actually I think the chances are very good: such men look after their skins first and always.'

The photograph showed five men left to right, standing at attention. It was a newspaper photograph, but not printed, which explained its quality. Kenneally wrote that it was taken on 20 December 1937, at the opening of the new Senior Course Academy buildings of the Japanese Army Academy at a place called Sagamihara. Matsui, Mori, Tsuji and Hattori, all together. A note said Emperor Hirohito had also been present, but was not in the picture.

The boy looked at the third man. Tall. Six feet or so, tall for them, Kenneally had commented. Bushy eyebrows, slight bald patch indistinctly seen. The eyes were expressionless, but this did not mean anything during an age when everybody posed stiffly, some even with hostility, for photographs. A flabby face which to the boy always suggested mother's darling.

The letter summed up Mori's career, which from all appearances had been steadily progressing since 1930, proving the old maxim that some men blossom—there is no other more incongruous word—during times of war.

But he was not a fighter, said the Military Intelligence man in the crisply typed *CV*, the short sentences evidence of practice at breaking down information into small bits for impatient senior officers. Planner. Successful, ambitious, connected. Known for coming up with unexpected ideas; as many surprises as a fox with the hounds after him.

His difference from his colleagues was best shown in his choice of ceremonial wear, someone had noted on the file. The boy could see what he wore clearly enough on the photograph.

'He won't be where we will look for him, so we will look for him elsewhere and he will not be there either,' wrote Kenneally, either in self-pity or a hangover. 'Definitely has problems with Kotoku Sato, commanding officer of the Division, but is close to General Mutaguchi, who commands their 15th Army and is the overall commander of their Burma offensive. Rumoured to be paranoid about personal safety, as he should be, the sod. Does that satisfy your academic curiosity?'

Bartlett had done the explaining to Rajkhowa as soon as he got the letter and the photograph.

'Now look here,' he said to him that morning after calling him in. 'You have to go back home; there is no help for it. There is no reason for me to stop you. There will be no exams this summer, nor at the year's end, from what I hear.

'I could tell you I know something of how you feel at the moment, but you know I do. I was only a little older than you when I enlisted in '14. So many boys my age who I knew never returned from that war.

'Now, you might think you are here, safe and sound, and your friend is dead. You might be thinking what you can do about it. His grandfather and yours wanted you to find out about this business, so now you will go and tell them what you have found. That is your part.

'That old Naga is the craftiest fox I have seen in these parts, and if I know a bit about the way he thinks, he is planning something. All I can say is: whatever it is, stay out of it. You are a good student, and you have many gifts. After this war, things will settle down, and who knows where this country and your people will go. You have a part in all that, so when you go home, remember it.

'The Army has been informed of this Japanese Colonel, so perhaps we might see justice served to him when he is caught. There is nothing more we can do, is there?'

'No, sir.'

By which he meant: *I can't think of anything more to do. At the moment.*

He had packed then, putting a few clothes into a tarpaulin satchel and refusing Mopumeren's offer to carry it for him. He had a thorough and uncharacteristically passionate dislike for tin trunks, those monstrous boxes in which people carried what seemed to be their entire households on board trains and ferries.

He said goodbye to Henderson and the other boys, telling them a vague tale of somebody unwell at home, and walked out to the drive where a *tonga* would take him to the ferry.

The headmaster had thought of offering his car, but guessed, correctly, that boys like these took their proximity to authority as a matter of course and did not like advertising it. The headmaster watched them leave, wondering if his parting advice would be followed, sad and certain in equal parts that it might not. Then he remembered that he was a man of the cloth, so he sent up a prayer.

*

Meren came up to the roof and sat beside him. On the evening of the first day Gojen had explained in detail what he had found. The man had listened without a question or gesture, and told him to tell all that to the *burha*s, the old men. A chain of command was being set already. The boy did not bother asking what they were thinking about back home. If they could wait for him, he could likewise.

Towards dawn the next day they reached Gauhati, crossing the deep swamp-banks to its west. The boy did not like the town as it was then, a courthouse and a settlement along its banks and scattered villages inland. Everyone else said Gauhati would soon come into its own if only somebody drained the swamps.

The river here narrowed till it was little more than a mile across. This narrow stretch was the reason why the place was special for the boy. In 1671, the great Ahom general Lachit Borphukan had built a system of earthen walls or *garh*s from hill to hill on both banks. Aurangzeb's Mughal army under the Rajput Ram Singh had been thwarted in an open battle and cut down by malaria and other diseases rising from the swamps. The invaders had at last chosen the river to push forward, and here the smaller, faster boats of the Ahom navy had run circles round them and simply disintegrated the Mughals.

It was a good story, and the boy liked it because it was consistent with his ideas on mobility and flexibility as he had learnt during his time with the Nagas. In the dawn, however, he slept through Gauhati, after a dinner of rice and *xaak*, a special meal from the ferry's crew, but which he had picked at without interest. He didn't sleep well either, but dreamt of ferns.

*

It was early afternoon on day ten, and the ferry had made good time coming upriver. The rains had not begun in earnest and the river could still be navigated well.

He stood some distance away from the edge of the ferry's bridge, Mopumeren keeping a lookout in case someone they knew was at the dock and they had to avoid him. This was Neamatighat, the dock at Jorhat. It was a line of smooth mudbanks where the silt had not piled up over the winter. The riverbed here rose up steeply, so the large ferries stayed mid-river and passengers were rowed to the bank.

The boy and the man got off and walked up the bank. There was a small market at the verge which they crossed furtively. At the other end and off the road, the boy told the Naga to go on ahead and he would follow later.

Gojen's idea was to avoid as much of Jorhat town (spelt, naturally, Jorhaut by the British) as he could. He liked the town, with its neat streets and clean houses, the well-mannered people and the aura of culture and civility. At one time or the other in his life, it generally appeared as if half of Jorhat knew him by face or was related in some way.

This was partly true. The Rajkhowas were all over the town; there were three plantations southward near the hills, a doctor, a judge, timber mills near Dibrugarh to the east. Another uncle was into materials' supplies for the Army; that genius had beaten all family expectations by running— so far—at substantial loss, unheard of during a war. Each part of town swarmed with his uncles, aunts and cousins, always eager to ask him everything, taking special delight in what they thought was a promising boy at last. At the moment, though, the boy in question wanted no one to ask him anything at all.

Taking off his shirt in the humid afternoon, he walked south from the river to the crossroads, where the Assam Trunk Road, going east, met the river road coming south. From here he went south again, slinging the satchel on his left shoulder and his shirt on the right, in a long oblique line taking him as south and east of the town as it could.

Planter's Store approached, and here Gojen, called 'Ginger' by the elderly Anglo who ran it, went off the road near a mud culvert and across the meadows. It wasn't the name: he was used to it being mauled by his schoolmates. They sometimes called him 'Gin' and this was fine by him too. Sometime earlier, a proposal to call him Gaijin was taken up after the Brits discovered what the Japs called *them*. This, however, was quickly shot down after a countermotion questioned what his fists might do to the first boy who called him that.

He did not mind Planter's, where he could get all the good things he preferred, including strawberry jam, all kinds of new tinned food that the war had brought in and new 'scientific' objects, nor the Anglo's daughter, who was about his age and who he thought interesting, in parts. But he did not want to meet any of the British who bought their supplies from the store, most of whom knew his people.

Two aircraft rose beyond the trees, flying close one behind the other, banked and headed south-east. They were too far away to recognise, but were probably Royal Air Force Hurricanes (they were too small for supply planes), though they could also be some of the new American planes he had heard were based out of RAF Station Jorhat. They would be on a bombing mission in the hills, even in Burma. He had a vague notion that war involved much bombing and dust and smoke and noise.

The war. It had been a constant beast, ever since the day his father and he were sitting at the magistrate's house, listening to a radio announcement about distant events and a declaration. Poland, France, Dunkirk, the bombings of London and in the east, China, Manchuria, Singapore. For a ten-year-old, it had appeared as though the war would be a perpetual event.

It had finally dawned on him that the war was inching (literally, on the map) closer, when 10,500 British and Indian refugees reached the Digboi-Ledo oil belt in East Assam in spring 1942. Their journey, barely days ahead of the Japanese, was one of incredible hardships from Maingkwan, deep in north-central Burma, through the Hukong Valley, Shinbwiyang and then through the Pangsau Pass, the narrow funnel of sheer hills from Burma that leads into easternmost Assam.

The armies of the world began converging on the plains of his land and drove east through the passes, the aircraft made their sorties, units of young white men drove through east, always east. Naturally, his physical world was limited to Jorhat and the hills of the Ao and he had thought the mountains to the east, the great Patkai Range, would always come between the world he knew and the war he had heard about. This had always been a fixed belief. But the war had finally crept across ...

He went in a straight line across the fields, his school shoes sinking into the mud in a few places or splashing small puddles in the grass. Sowing would begin shortly, but it had begun raining from the look of things.

The villages here were mud or half-brick, with tin roofs or thatch, each house with a row of betel nut trees around it. The villages were usually at the centre of their fields.

He stopped at one of the large ponds to be found near the villages. These were square and dug deep, sometimes to twenty feet, to make a constant source of water, fish and duck pond combined. The water level varied with the rains, but was about five feet from the brim just then. He walked down the mudbank to a grassy patch near the surface, unslung his satchel, threw down his shirt, sat down and took his shoes off.

Across the meadows of Assam grows a type of grass that in appearance is like a reed, but is grass nevertheless. Very narrow-stemmed and ranging in height from six inches to a foot, it has on its head a bristle of tiny seeds. This is the *bon* seed, and its purpose is twofold. The first is to stick as tenaciously as it can, in its hundreds, to the clothes of anyone who walks through the meadows, and to take them off later is a lesson in patience and dexterity.

The other is to be chewed at the stem by boys in the late

spring with much, or nothing, on their minds. Our boy, as he plucked the *bon* seeds from his socks and slid his bare feet through the pond water into the cool mud, had much on his mind.

His was a close extended family, with everyone at almost an equal social level, which makes getting along easier. He was on comfortable terms with cousins his age. His two brothers, being older, did not count. But Uti was different.

He had known Uti all his life, just as his father had known Uti's and his grandfather knew Shilukaba. It had started when K. C. Rajkhowa, his grandfather, had first met the Naga at Amguri down the road from Jorhat towards the Naga Hills. It was a friendship born of an equal love for the hills and respect for each other, for Shilukaba was from an old family too, and a man held in immense respect in his tribe.

So the generations had grown closer as Shilukaba tried to give a sense of direction to his people and times changed. Gojen remembered Uti's mother and the stories she used to tell when he visited them at Amguri, where the old man held a provisional court of sorts for his people together with the district magistrate of the area.

Uti's mother had died shortly after his father, both from cholera, when the boys were nine. Rajkhowa's mother had been like a mother to Uti afterwards, and Uti stayed at the plantation as much as his grandfather allowed.

A duck waddled across the pond and looked at Gojen but lost interest and went away, quacking duck questions.

The boy remembered Uti as he best remembered him: the small-boned light frame dancing around him, teasing. 'Elephant-boy, *hati lora*, elephant-boy,' he would sing, darting in and pinching his cheeks and daring him to chase. For the truth was, Gojen had been a very rotund little boy with cheeks that everyone loved pulling, and short stout legs that were not much use for running. Someone—Rajkhowa was sure it was his grandfather—had told Uti what his name meant. King of Elephants. And so *hati* was what he was called.

'Uti *aru hati*,' the Naga boy would say. Uti and his elephant, and the elephant chased the boy for much of his early childhood until he lost the baby fat but the only name Gojen could think up for his friend was 'Owl-nose'.

They would walk through meadows like these, and hills like those beyond, and when they were ten, Gojen was asked by Shilukaba if he would like to go with Uti to the *morung*. This was the boys' dormitory in every Naga village, a time of learning the oral traditions of their people, of learning the ways of the village and the forest, a rite of passage that was important to Uti and his grandfather, an inheritance not to be taken lightly.

So Rajkhowa had gone and stayed for six whole months, his grandfather approving, his father secretly envious because *he* had not been invited when he was little, and everyone else in the family aghast.

Gojen had gone to the *morung* a former elephant and returned something else, for there he found company, with boys his age and the elders. He learnt their stories and legends, the old way of life, the customs by which their people had lived for ages and more than anything else, the secrets of the forest. Here he found he adapted and learnt quicker than most the art of tracking, living off the land, hunting for food. Uti was better, of course, quicker, sharper, more athletic, but the boys had come to a provisional truce and did not pull each other's legs in front of the others.

They learnt how to spin tops or *mezung*; they built stilts to race each other; they even had bull-roarer whistles (though some whistles sounded more like frogs croaking).

34

They sneaked up behind the elders' backs and blew the huge hollow-log gongs in the village. These gongs were broadcast instruments of old and it had been great fun to make a noise and startle everyone in the middle of the day, for the noise the gongs made was simply tremendous.

At night they would lie under the stars on the platform built on stilts outside the *morung*, talking of this and that, and arguing about the legends. Each had his fixed views on these matters. For Uti, everything that was told must have happened, otherwise why would anyone tell it? For Gojen, who knew much fiction from his grandfather, anything that was possible *might* have happened, but not everything anyone said was possible. For him the truth lay in the forest, in what he saw, felt or heard. Beyond that anything was not worth much considering.

Gojen came back from the *morung* and was sent straight to school, his grandmother having won a significant victory over her husband about the boy's future. Generations of Rajkhowas had gone to Bengal, she had told him during one especially bloody skirmish, but her Gojen was going to be somebody and not come back and become a 'moss-covered planter', as she put it.

So the boy had gone, but he returned each year, and Uti and his elephant were together again, at the house, in the fields and meadows, pulling the most fearsome pranks and, in the forests and swamps, with other men of their families, learning about the world and discovering themselves. Gojen also went to the *morung* twice later, and sat in when Uti was introduced to the tribe elders as the person to lead them later in all matters. And in the one element where Gojen was unmatched, Uti would look at him now and then, saying 'Fat Boy, you might have something good in you after all.'

If he could imagine himself crying, he would. If he could cry now, he would, because there was such an ache in his heart and a feeling of the loss that men only feel for their brothers, and no one else.

The worst part was the ache would not go away and he did not know what to do. He did not know of anything he could do, for the first time in his life: a till now unimagined feeling of helplessness, because he was one of those who waded right in and solved problems as they came up. And with that helplessness, a heavy chill was lodging deeper and deeper in his heart, permanently, relentlessly.

He chewed the last of half-a-dozen *bon* stalks, tied the shoelaces together and wore his shoes around his neck, putting the socks inside the satchel and the shirt on his shoulder again.

It was nearing evening when he reached the northern edge of the estate and saw the rows of tea plants slanting over the horizon. He could take the main road through the front gates but decided to walk around the fence to a smaller gate which led directly to the house. This was a quarter mile down the road. He passed a few tea labour women coming down the estate road, their baskets on their backs, the rope balanced on a wad of cloth on their heads.

There was not much picking at the estate now. As in other matters, the war had hit here as well. Blitz or not, Londoners still needed their tea, but the cost of transporting it and the losses along the way had affected everybody. Most estates, like this, which had other businesses to support it, were trying to roll with the punches.

He edged past a small gap in the fence, walking the pickers' path along the tea plants under the evening shade of the trees that at intervals shaded the tea plants, along the edge of the deep drainage gullies which criss-crossed the

36

plantation, forming a circuitous route to the house. He was as close to being terrified as he had ever come in his short but active life.

It wasn't snakes or leeches or boars or his parents. His father was a constant but harmless puzzle, and his mother was a patient, kind and well-bred woman who everyone acknowledged was far more intelligent and had more common sense than her husband.

It was his grandmother. That lady was, in Gojen's eyes, not human, but a creature of steel and fire. Sure, a dear and loving grandmotherly figure, if left alone, given to reading the scriptures and encouraging 'culture' among the relatives in between entertaining the British and Indian planters. But a life spent with old KC had made her impatient with what she called 'foolish schemes', and anyone not walking the straight and narrow would come up against her and get blown apart. If he walked into the house now, out of the blue, during term, no matter what the reason might be, he would be spending the rest of the summer picking up small parts of himself.

So he came up at the garden fence nearest the pond and the lawn where they had breakfast sometimes, looked around cautiously, stepped up to the wooden post between the steel mesh and jumped down on the other side.

It was getting dark now, and he edged slowly along the fence, not stepping on the lawn, looking at the windows and the back veranda. He caught a whiff of a familiar smell from somewhere. He reached a tree and stepped to the side.

'She is not here.'

His grandfather, in trousers, shirt and grey moustache, was sitting at the base of the tree on a cane chair, stuffing —and the boy's heart lightened when he saw it—a clay stem pipe. It was a very British fad the old man had picked up and continued through sheer force of will for at least three decades. It was also a signal: if he was relaxed enough to smoke the foul tobacco, it meant his wife was absent.

'*Koka.*' The boy sat down next to him, but not that close, plucked up a *bon* stem and chewed it.

'She is not here, so you need not creep around the garden like a *sika*. I need not, either.' *Sika* is Assamese for the Indian musk shrew, or *chhuchhunder*, referring in most Indian languages to furtive—and smelly—people. The old man had colourful imagery, part of the humour he had built up after each combat loss to his wife.

'What good are you if you could not smell the tobacco?'

'But she will return.'

'Not soon enough. I told your mother the two of them could go to the town and stay somewhere for a few days. I told them Shiluka and I would like to be left alone for now, and they would feel better not having to talk to him. They are at your uncle's.'

'Father?'

'Still at Dibrugarh. He won't return soon either.' At the timber mill seventy miles east. The mill was doing well during the war.

'What if they call at the school?'

KC glanced sideways. 'It took you ten days to think of that? You couldn't ask me, when you phoned to say you were leaving, what would happen if your parents or your grandmother knew you were coming back?'

Actually, it had been a constant thought, but pushed behind.

'*Koka*, if they call ...'

'How many telephones are there in Jorhat, if they are working, that is?'

The boy thought, maybe four that he knew of: modern

curiosities for those who could afford them, but not of much practical use. There was one at the magistrate's court and jail, but he could not imagine his stately grandmother walking through the convicts, not even to call him.

'Light of my clan, all phone connections in Upper Assam pass through Jorhat.'

'So?'

'So I bribed that Gogoi operator and his assistant not to connect any calls to your school from anywhere here. Except Jorhat 6. And that is …'

'Ours.'

The boy relaxed a little. It was sometimes an advantage to have a grandfather who had occasionally deep pockets, a taste for dark conspiracy, shared your views on the authorities and who did not have anything resembling a conscience when it came to you.

'Gogoi operator asked for ten rupees, but I got him down to seven. I don't understand why he thinks he is so important, all he does is push a stick here, plug it there. He even gets to listen to all the gossip.'

'*Seven* rupees? That is a lot of money.'

'More than he earns in three months, I think. Then I had to pay his assistant another seven to keep an eye on him.'

Talking of other matters, staying away from the issue.

'Where is Shilukaba?'

'He went out to meet someone shortly before Meren came in. He said he would return late at night.'

'How is he?'

'Meeting people. Meeting a whole lot of people. There is a lot of activity going on. You'll find out. Otherwise, I don't know. I have never seen him like this, not even when his son died. Sometimes he sits here with me and talks about Uti and you. He is waiting for you.' He glanced sideways again.

'Did you get everything, like you said?'

'The headmaster knew someone in the Army who has written everything the British know. And I ...'

'Tell it to Shiluka and me together later. This was Bartlett, wasn't it?'

'Yes.'

'He must have told you something. Your leaving in the middle of the term, all that.'

'He told me it was all right because he had been here and understood. He told me not to get involved in anything other than telling you what I found.'

'Be careful of middle-aged British men who encourage you too much.'

'*Koka* ...'

'Not to get involved. We have a lot to think about, Shiluka and I. You did your part.'

'What is going to happen?'

'Haven't you heard?'

No, he had been on a boat in the middle of the river for ten days, hadn't he?

'The Japanese are at Kohima.'

'When? They captured it?'

'Five days ago. They are still fighting the British there. They also attacked near Dimapur.'

Closer. They were closer. Dimapur was on the plains this side of the hills.

'What will happen?'

'I don't know,' said his grandfather, worry showing through at last. 'The British are bombing them and still fighting in Burma. They want to stop them in the hills, I think. If the British retreat, I really can't say what will happen. Maybe you should have stayed in Calcutta.'

'What are Shilukaba and his people doing?'

'Everyone has left the hills. They say all the villages on Kohima Ridge are empty. That is Angami land, but even the other tribes are moving out. A few of Shiluka's elders came here, about a fortnight ago. Now they are to send some young men, talk about things. This is more than a tragedy for them. It is bad enough the villagers were murdered like that. It's a crisis. Shiluka's family is vital in many ways to the tribe. About what they will do, everything depends on what he thinks about your information. Anyway, now that you are here, what will you do?'

The boy thought about this. It wasn't much to think about, anyhow. There was no Uti, so he had only the other recourse.

'My boxes are still in my room?'

His grandfather turned towards him again, and there was a gleam of another time in his eyes.

3

In a few ways, hunting with a rifle is like swimming. In most other ways, it is like nothing else most humans do. Like the swimmer's first contact with water, the first contact with a good rifle is like an introduction to a new element, a new force partly frightening, partly overwhelming in its possibilities. Like the good swimmer, the truly gifted hunter gets over this alien fascination very quickly: those who confess to be fascinated with either water or guns are frequently those who should not be permitted anything to do with either.

From fascination to understanding is the next logical, and therefore most difficult, step. It involves as much understanding of physical laws and mechanics as understanding oneself. Once the mechanics are mastered, the possibilities of what can be done with this new element open up.

Gojen was ten when he first inserted a pellet into a little lever-operated air rifle with a long, heavy iron barrel, a rough finish and almost no polish at all. The first time he squeezed the trigger he felt the short, vicious recoil on his shoulderblade, his grandfather saying, 'Good, now you know. Now try to hit something.'

From that first pellet—whose diameter, as he learnt later, was 22/100th of an inch and therefore called a .22 calibre—to a bigger rifle was a gradual process. The first lesson which everyone seems to know but few really master —squeeze, don't pull the trigger—was a deceptively simple one, growing more complicated. Which part of the finger to squeeze with? Just how much should he squeeze? Where should he look? How? Which was the best way to hold the rifle? Which was the best way to stand? Or sit, or kneel?

On autumn dawns he started going with old KC, Shilukaba and Uti to the swamps west of the estate, the mist coming in from the river, cold and damp. The hunting trips, mostly for birds, were considered sport by the men of the family and good hospitality if there were Indian or English guests. Besides, in areas bordering strips of wild forest, rifles are very useful to protect life and land. Sometimes neighbouring planters joined in.

On one such trip, Shilukaba had asked in an aside to the boy: 'Do you know the difference between this and our tribesmen's hunting in the hills?'

And when Gojen could not reply to this, the old Naga had said: 'In the hills, they hunt for food. Sometimes they go out for a long while, not knowing for certain if they will get anything to feed their families. They have to be very careful because a lot depends on how good they are. They take much difficulty in getting the kill. People here get good food anyway: it does not cost much for you. People like you, like the Ingraz, hunt because it is fun. Specially the Ingraz: they hunt with people who scare the game out into the open, with dogs and drums. The Ingraz sits in a comfortable place and the scared animal just runs out to be shot so that the man can take the skin home and tell his friends what a good hunter he is. I have shown so many big men, white and brown, how to hunt, and none of them deserved their kills.'

The boy had thought this over and asked the old man, 'Then how can I deserve it?'

The old man had said: by not making things easy, by not having bearers and dogs to do your work for you, by becoming a part of the swamps and taking as much discomfort as the birds you hunt live with. By making yourself and the birds as equals.

Chewing over this piece of valuable advice, the boy and Uti started going out on their own on autumn dawns, wading through the marshes in the cold, standing as still as they could in the freezing water, waiting for the birds. It was different.

When he was twelve and already a big-sized boy, he got his first deer. It was a small swamp deer, out in a tiny grass patch between the swamps and the river. Swamp deer liked such grass patches, he had been told. They were predictable and patterns always worked to the hunter's advantage.

He had waited, standing thigh-deep in dirty water full of *meteka* or swamp hyacinth, waited nearly an hour in the windless stillness till the deer had come, looking straight ahead and not seeing him. That time, he had got it exactly as he had been told, with the deer facing him, a little to the side, the bullet striking the bony joint between the neck and the back, the cleanest way to bring down an animal of that size.

He had given the animal to Uti and his people, and they had a little feast for his first great shot and how he had got it, and why. There were two lessons he learnt that day. The first was: the only reason to hunt something was to eat it, or to take an animal for those who deserved such good food. The second was: grass-eating animals cannot see you unless you move or they smell you, because by the nature of how their eyes are placed on different sides of their head, they cannot see distances.

He had learnt about stereoscopic vision two whole years before he was taught this in school.

By his second deer, a little more than a year later, his lessons at the *morung* had progressed, and he began combining forest-craft with shooting, going up into the hills with his father, grandfather and the Nagas. Around this time he had been gifted a wholly better rifle, this one a 1927 Lee-Enfield Mark III, a year older than him, which meant in those parts state-of-the-art.

With this he became more involved in the mechanics of shooting, the numerous small and perfectly cooperating parts of the instrument, the function of each and their meaning.

For some time, KC had a small range of sorts far inside the estate, in a deep hollow among the tea shrubs. On one side were four targets, backed by a deep line of compressed straw and mud. The targets were in hard cardboard, bought from elsewhere and, after KC's nephew went into Army supplies, from the surplus store. The cardboard was held in place by iron hooks on each side, the distances from the firing platform carefully measured out, for the Jorhat Gentlemen's Rifle Club—as the pot-bellied planters, British and Indian, grandly called themselves—were very particular in their preferences. The guns were mostly bolt action rifles and of medium calibre, from .300 onward. The targets were at 75, 100, 150 and 200 yards. Beyond that, they said, they were not interested.

At those distances, however, they were, in one word, laughable. They would gather on a day—any day was suitable, because all they did through the week was live at their estates with hardly anything interesting happening unless an elephant crashed into the tea plantations—and spend a lot of time under the tin shelter of the firing platform, running their hands over their gleaming guns, fingering their cartridges.

Occasionally one or the other would stand or kneel or fire prone at the targets. Their accuracy was not even proportionate to the distance of the targets. Occasionally, one of them would find either of the two inner circles or the deep cross at the centre. This was more a matter of chance than will or consistency. Such events were a cause for much discussion and celebration.

Gojen was usually there, watching his grandfather's guests amusing themselves, wondering why they were not any more accurate than they seemed to be. On some afternoons he would come up here alone or with KC and practise.

Then one day, Fuller, the old widower from the next plantation, who was very keen about guns and one of the few who paid any attention to their shots, beckoned him over and said, 'You have a very fine gun there. Do you want to take a shot?' Fuller had just put in one at 150 yards into the deep cross.

The boy went to the platform, lay down on the hard board across from the 100-yard, and put five from the Lee-Enfield into the deep cross. Fuller went down to the cardboard, unhooked it, and brought back an uneven rectangle of dots on the four arms of the cross, with the centre dot almost at the exact centre of the cross.

'This,' the planter had said with a sigh and some inaccuracy, 'is what we call a diamond. Well played, my boy.' And the incident had passed, but not without old KC being patted on the back by the other men.

Fuller would return often and spent a deal of time with the boy, telling him where to refine his firing position, and teaching him all the theoretical parts of shooting he didn't know. This included the nature of the bullets, how much difference their weight and the weight of the powder inside a live cartridge made to the shooting, what difference the angle of fire and posture of the body made to the overall steadiness of the shot. These were things Fuller knew, and he also knew that he could not be what the boy was naturally built to be: consistent.

And consistent was what Gojen was busy becoming. The diamond pattern grew tighter and tighter on the cross, the shots got closer to one another, and he began shooting at the more distant targets. He learnt that in America, where people were more serious about guns than the British were, target shooters had a different term for this: clover leaf, the pattern which the shots resembled, a kind of leaf that was difficult to get and considered lucky. So was the pattern.

Backed by the occasional book on riflemanship Gojen borrowed from his neighbours, he began entering notes in a small hardcover notebook, with calculations and studies: this was about the time he discovered that he had a natural head for numbers and measurements and much better sight than most. He learnt more about his body, the feel when he made an accurate shot, the way his body had been placed, the memory of his bones and muscles.

He learnt about such concepts of physics as muzzle velocity, the difference made by gravity to the accuracy of the shot and about trajectories. He learnt a bit about chemistry too, from the super-fast expansion of the powder inside a live cartridge when it is struck by the firing pin, the process which pushes the bullet forward. It took him some time and a lot of errors and discomfort, but by the end, he really *knew* what he was doing.

*

It was now the morning after he arrived. He had not gone running at dawn. He was at the range, with the Lee-Enfield, half a box of cartridges, a glass bottle of Spencer's Gun Cleaner—a fluid which was difficult to get and which KC had told him to use sparingly—a ramrod and a flannel rag, rolls of hospital cotton, a wooden ruler, a protractor and his notebook. The sun was coming up in a mild way, and it was cool in the hollow. He was lying on his bare stomach on one of the boards at the firing platform, which was angled a little upwards and level with the targets. The gun rested on a sack of thickly packed sand, which kept it steady but prevented the barrel from shuddering with the recoil.

His legs were stretched straight and a little wide behind him, and he was wearing shoes so his toes would not bend, because he had discovered that if they stayed bent inward for too long —which happened in this position—they started quivering.

The long stock of the rifle was pressed against the plate-like muscles which were beginning to form between his upper right chest and shoulders. His left hand was stretched straight against the platform and held up the barrel in the centre of his palm. The elbow was hard against the platform. He was looking along the rear sight, a pointed knob in this older version of the rifle, down to the front sight, a trident; the rear knob and central spike of the trident on the edge of the barrel lining up against the centre of the cross on the target, which at this distance was just barely distinct, but distinct nonetheless. His short neck was still, his left eye closed, his right eye on the front sight. At this distance, he had discovered—with a little prodding from Fuller—that

48

he need not hold half his breath in, because for an accurate shooter, that much stillness of the upper body, for that distance, came naturally. Competition shooters, he had been told, considered this distance barely worth the bother.

He remembered something the planter had told him at his house, a quote by a famous American competition shooter. That gent had remarked once, according to the papers: '*Two* hundred yards? Why, at that range, I don't need a rifle. I might as well punch the target down.'

Gojen suppressed a little smile at the thought of such marvels, looked down the sight, saw the blur of the cross against the central spike of the trident and squeezed back with the ball of his right index finger. The trigger came back in a smooth movement, reached nearly the halfway point where it suddenly became tense, refusing to be pushed further. The ball of the finger pushed back just a little more, the tension broke, the boy could not see the cross for a moment and smoke flared across the sight. He heard the muffled—but still sharp—boom and felt the recoil against his shoulder.

With the upper centre of his right palm, he grabbed the rounded bolt head, pulled it back horizontally, pushed it down vertically, pulled it up vertically and pushed it forward horizontally, hearing the click of the next cartridge settling into the chamber, the four-fold action of the bolt familiar, comforting. He sighted again and fired. The whole action from firing once to chambering a fresh round to firing again, if he had timed himself—he would have to get a stopwatch from the Anglo when he could get the money from KC—would have been a second and three-quarters.

The magazine was a double-column, a very modern system, though he preferred using only five rounds at a time. Part of the practice also involved, as he told himself, improving his reloading and re-chambering time: the time it took to eject a spent cartridge and insert a fresh one. His speed at this was good, but at the back of his mind all the time was the name of Sergeant Instructor Snoxall. Thirty years earlier, with the same rifle but a different model, Snoxall had chambered, reloaded and fired thirty-eight shots into a *twelve-inch* target at 300 yards in *one minute*. It must have seemed like a machine gun firing, or one of those new automatic Sten guns he had seen with British infantrymen once when he was visiting the Jorhat RAF airbase. It was a world record in aimed bolt-action rifle shooting that the boy was sure would stay around for some time.

The five shots were not exactly in a diamond, he knew before he reached the target. The left was a little above the horizontal line and outside the cluster made by the other four, distorting the invisible rectangle that would otherwise have formed.

He brought back the piece of paper and spread it on the platform, taking the ruler and compass and measuring the distance between the holes. If it weren't for the fifth one, the distance between the four arms of the diamond would be an even 4.8 inches, with the centre hole halfway in between.

He pulled out the thick rolls of cotton he had stuffed into his ears as Meren, who had been sitting on a bench some distance away, came over and looked at the paper. The Naga too was pulling cotton rolls out of his ears.

'Not good. Like always.'

'Yes. It is always wrong the first time after I return.'

'But the other holes are closer than before.'

'No. See …' the boy said, showing the calculations from the winter before. 'They are further away than before. I need to practise more.'

Meren looked again at the numbers. He had a bit of church education and a lot of practical knowledge, but he couldn't see why such a small difference mattered. 'It is still better than anyone else.'

Not good enough, the boy thought. The idea of shooting smaller and smaller diamonds at longer and longer distances was an overpowering drug, better even than waiting for birds in the swamps. He would never hunt again now, without his brother.

'Maybe you should run a bit, feel better.'

'No. I'll just have to practise.'

He stuffed the roll of cotton back into his ears, went to the other board across from the 100-yard target, lay down and brought the rifle up, putting five more rounds into the small magazine, working the bolt. He would have to go back to the small beginning, the shorter distance. He would have to get better, if he was to feel less useless.

Meren went back to his post, insulating his ears likewise. This was a treat, he always considered. He had done some rough things when he was younger, and could use a rifle, had hunted with spear and crossbow and had been to war, a real war, long ago. But to sit and watch the boy doing something as bizarre and boring as lying down and shooting and measuring and getting agitated over inches was a curiously fascinating sight.

Gojen's mind had turned to the cartridges. He liked the Lee-Enfield. Everyone uniformly seemed to agree that it was a good rifle: a hunter's rifle and a shooter's rifle, dependable and accurate. The Mark III model had begun life in 1907, a better-designed version of the older models. It had a five-round magazine, and was officially known as the Short Magazine Lee-Enfield, or SMLE. Tommies in the First World War, who found much reason to be thankful to it, had begun calling it Emily after the acronym.

The one in the boy's hand fired .303 calibre rounds, the 180-grain bullet of lead pushed out by rapidly expanding black powder with a muzzle velocity of 2,437 feet per second and accuracy up to 250 yards, beyond which it began dropping a little, acted upon by the twin forces of friction and gravity.

This phenomenon was an exciting discovery for the boy, who reasoned—and was told he was correct—that the longer the distance, the more the bullet would fall. Therefore, to hit a target at vast distances, say at a great thousand-yard contest across the world called the Wimbledon Cup, the shooter would have to aim at a different spot. The difference would have to be made up by calculations based on the weight of the bullet, its velocity, the speed of the wind. It was like doing quadratic equations in a hollow deep inside a tea estate.

More reading had introduced him to iron sights, used by marksmen across the world, and to telescopic sights, which he would have given anything to see. So far, his work had told him the furthest limits of his reach. But within that limit, he knew almost all there was to know of the science and much of the art.

He chambered in another round, thinking somewhere of the fast little wild pig he and Uti had last hunted together near Mokokchung the previous winter. He fired again and chambered again ...

An estate employee had walked down into the hollow to his right and was gesturing. Gojen pulled out the tickly wads of cotton.

'The old man is back. We are to see him now, I think,' said Meren.

Practice would wait.

4

'*Ahili.*'

The man came out of some Ao legend, some dark and bloody epic of ceremony and combat, drumroll and fire. The man wore his past and all the spirits of his people had been called up. His eyes were blazing.

The Aos are an ancient people, even in a land where ancient means *really* ancient and the histories of nations stretch far back through time. *Ao*, or *Aor*, in their language, they say, means 'those who came before', as opposed to *Mirir*, 'those who came afterwards': that is, the other tribes. The first-born, the eldest tribe of all the Naga tribes, some of whom live in the plains of Assam and many others, an entire tribe, in the mountains of north Burma.

Some others say *Ao* simply means 'those who are' and this may be equally true, for the ancient people of the world named themselves in their own context, like the Egyptians called their land *afru eika*, 'our land', from which the name of that continent derives.

In either case, the Aos have been around in their hills for ages, even as kingdoms rose and fell elsewhere in the plains of the Luit to the west, cultures were formed and changed, languages grew and books were written. They

53

were ancient when Ahom warriors under the legendary Su-ka-pha crossed their hills on their way from Burma to found a kingdom in Assam in the early thirteenth century.

The Aos went on with their lives, governed by their laws and overseen by a council of elders and chiefs, a stable tribal republic trading (and, on occasion, battling fiercely) with the other tribes and also with the plainsmen of Assam.

Ao lands were divided in four parts, each part a range or *kong*, the tribesmen identified by which range their villages fell under. Other identifiers were clan and family.

The Ao have many stories about the birth of their nation and the men who fuelled their rise and spread. Among them is the story of their greatest warrior and chief, leader of their first raid, whose marvellous exploits passed on into virtually every aspect of their ceremonies and customs. The Pongen clan, descended from that warrior, is the eldest and the most revered of all the families.

Shilukaba was from this clan, scion of an almost-holy lineage.

He had been born a Baptist, as the Church had come to the hills in his father's time. He had been taught by English preachers and knew the Bible. He took the better parts of this influence and had little time for the rest. In a private conversation he had once said: Jesus was definitely a great man, but he would have had a difficult time in the hills. The pastor was a younger Ao, and wise. He had not disputed this.

The boy had always remembered him as a modest, dignified old man, even humorous, always ready with impeccable advice on the ways of the world and the forest, always mindful of his role among his people, always watchful about the Ingraz and their rule. Always urging placidity and reason above everything else, his outward

54

calmness seemingly undisturbed by the death of his son and daughter-in-law earlier. But that had been then.

'*Ahili.*'

Each of the almost two dozen Naga tribes speak a different dialect. Some are so completely different that communicating effectively was always an obstacle, which might have led to a lot of the wars which happened in earlier times, when villages of different tribes lived uncomfortably next to each other. The geographical areas of influence of each tribe were clearly defined, but still, there was always some hamlet or the other which found itself with another tribe as neighbour.

Over the years, the Nagas had managed to evolve a solution to this: a common language they called Nagamese, a mix of Assamese and some words or phrases common among the tribes. Nagamese, by nature, is a colourful language with colloquial grammar, and one of its features is a complete absence of the respectful second-person pronoun *apuni*, Assamese for *aap*, replaced by the diminutive *toi*, the plainsman's *tu*. For the Naga, anyone spoken to, elder or younger, in Nagamese, was a *tu*. And so:

'*Ahili.*' You have come.

This to the boy as he came up the garden, vaulting his mother's flowerbeds to the front steps of the house where the Ao chief sat waiting for him.

Shilukaba was in full ceremonial robes. Two boar tusks gleamed in an elaborate neckband, the ends tapering right to left along his throat, the broad ends held by clasps of metal and wood travelling around the back of his neck. He wore ceremonial earrings in the three piercings on his ears, brass and wood gauntlets and armbands. Across his body were the tattoos of his position: four vertical lines on the chin, a chain of lozenges from the throat to the bottom of the breast bone, inverted on the front of the shoulders and stomach, lozenges and solid squares on the wrists, lozenges on the lower part of the leg, and a sort of arrow pattern on the knee. He had once told the boy that it had taken five years to complete it, a ritual of passage that Uti was to have gone through soon. He had grey but thick hair and the shawl touched off the complete blackness in his eyes.

The shawl. Gojen had seen him with the shawl just once before, when Uti was introduced to the tribal council. It was a striking creation of alternate narrow bands of dark blue and red, with a few light blue lines travelling the length. All over it were thick long bunches of dog's fur dyed red, and it was edged at the ends with black and red goat's hair tassels, each tassel ornamented with corries and shells and it was *never* worn lightly. It was the only piece of cloth he had ever seen which spoke to those in its presence. What it said was: I was worn by the chief and by the sons of chiefs going back to the dawn of time, so listen when he speaks, hear his words and understand. Or something to that effect.

And in plain unvarnished sentences, Gojen had narrated all. They had sat there for some time, not looking at each other, and the old chief had asked him various questions, asked the boy his views on Kenneally's information and the character sketch of the Japanese officer. They had not talked about anything from the past, for the time had not come to bring it up.

The clearest realisation that everything he knew had changed came to the boy when they rose up from the steps. Uti's grandfather hesitated, turned, looked at him for a moment, embraced him awkwardly and walked away without a word. This from a man who, in the boy's conscious memory, had *never* touched anyone, for it was considered in some circles to be impolite.

Later that day came a formal council of sorts.

They were seated in KC's study on the ground floor of the house, the windows open and a gentle breeze going around. They were gathered in cane chairs and stools or *murha*s around a brick fireplace which never saw use except for very special guests or if it got really cold.

There were five other Nagas there, including Meren, who, being Shilukaba's torch-bearer and factotum, had to be there. Two others, sons of chiefs, were also known: Subongmeiba and Yajanlem. Gojen was expecting another man to be there as well: after Uti, his closest friend and teacher from his days in the *morung*, an incredible hunter and athlete, but he wasn't there. KC and the boy completed the group circled around the chief.

What Gojen could not understand was the Konyak.

'What is he doing here?' he had asked Meren before they gathered in the room, when he had seen who the guests were. The Konyak had been lounging on the veranda, looking out at the estate in a distant way.

'Who?'

'*Him*. The Konyak.'

Konyaks are a tribe from the northern Burmese mountains. Geographically, they are neighbours of the Ao. But relations between the two had been strained through wars and minor village disputes and they tended to avoid one another as far as possible. Having a Konyak Naga at a council was unthinkable.

Meren considered this question.

'Times are changing. The Konyak were the first of us to be invaded by the Japani. There are many of them in Assam now. They all left before the soldiers. You know that.'

'Yes, but this is a council. What is he doing at a council?'

Meren looked at him with his fixed, unblinking stare.

'His wife and children were killed in his village back there. He has been living in Amguri since then. He doesn't have anywhere to go. He knows us and we know him. When he heard what happened, he said he wanted to help. We couldn't refuse. What could we do? He sits there in Amguri, does not talk much, does some odd jobs wherever he can find any. He did not even join the scouts working for the Ingraz. What could we do?'

Times must be really changing, the boy thought. The tribes were coming together, crossing divides.

The Ao chief looked at each of the faces around him, in turn. The photograph he had been given was on a low table in the middle of the group. He was silent for a while, but when he spoke, in the formal manner he always used in gatherings, he was summing up everything.

'The Ao have lived in their hills since the day we came out of the earth at the Six Stones at Langterok. We have lived, we have fought, we have hunted and gathered and farmed and not a day has gone by when all the tribes of our people have not understood that the Ao are leaders and guides of men. Twenty-one years ago, a Baptist missionary, who neither knew nor cared about the Stones, broke one of them at Natsimi. I tried to make him understand, then. Today the Stones are all gone.'

He would pause and look at his listeners, occasionally gather his thoughts, finger the corries on his shawl, or stare at the photograph. If a man could look like a warrior and a tired old man at the same time, he was looking it.

'Why do I tell you this? We are all Christians now, as we shall continue to be. That is a different matter. But we are also a nation, we have our traditions and customs and ways of life from far beyond, before the Ingraz built their ships, maybe even before they started living in their brick houses.'

58

He looked at KC, who nodded.

'The times change in the hills. Yesterday the Ao were the greatest among the tribes. No one could stand before us. Today the Angami in the south have progressed well. The centre of the hills has shifted to Kohima; the Ingraz like those parts. That is all right, too. Tribes rise and decline. It does not trouble me too much.

'But the times change, and long ago I saw that the Ao would have to move with the times, but must also remember their past, for without it, they will only be moving forward to whatever they can get in the world, with nothing, no rock to hold on to.

'I had a son, my only son. Through him I wanted my people to move into the future with pride, carrying their traditions with them. To be a strong people once again. My son died. But he had a son, a grandson I was proud of. He understood what I meant for him and for my people. I named him Shiluti, after our greatest warrior and hero, and indeed he was like the Shiluti of legend, strong and wise, even when he was young. I saw a beautiful tomorrow for the Ao, with him to guide the people along.

'Today he is dead and so are eighty of our people, in a war that does not involve us. He was tied like an animal and killed slowly by the Japani. The war is between the Ingraz who came to our hills, like they came to these plains, and the Japani, who want what the Ingraz have. What does it matter to us? But the Japani killed our people, as they killed other tribesmen.' Now he was looking at the Konyak, who stared back, impassive.

'The Japani killed our people like animals, and they killed my Uti. They tied him to a cattle stake and cut him. The trackers say he killed two, maybe three Japani. He would have, I know.

'This boy here, who was brother to my grandson, has

brought news from the Ingraz in Calcutta. This is the man, this … Japani officer who, the Ingraz think, was responsible for the killing.' He passed the photograph along to his listeners.

'The Ingraz officer who gave this photograph does not know it is with us. He is supposed to know a lot about this man, the boy says. The man has been killing men, women and children in other countries far away, in China and in Burma. The Ingraz want him for these crimes, they say.

'If there is one word the Ingraz never tire of repeating to us, it is *justice*. No more fighting, they tell us. Now everyone will sit down and get justice, they say. Everyone will go to a court, stand before a judge and accuse the criminal. The criminal will be punished if the accuser *proves* his guilt, they say.

'Now this Ingraz officer says after the fighting is over, if the Japani lose, this monster will be caught and tried. The Ingraz have their courts and their systems and their lawyers. Maybe they will catch him, maybe he will be punished. And maybe some Ingraz lawyer in a court far away from here will prove to the judge that this man is innocent because no one saw him do it. How could they? *They are all dead.*

'But I know this, and you know this, that for the Ingraz, our men, women and children who were killed do not matter. They will say: Oh, these many natives were killed. It will be just a number for them. If it had been their people they would understand, but those who died were not theirs, they were *ours*.

'I am old. I am tired now. I will not wait for the Ingraz to sit down for their justice. I will not wait for this Japani to walk into a trial and laugh and make excuses. I want you to go to Kohima. All the Japani officers in the hills are at Kohima, fighting the Ingraz. There are many Naga scouts there, working for the Ingraz armies. I want you to go there as scouts, live in the hills, find out where the Japani officers are. Find this man. The boy says he will not die fighting like a soldier. That is good. I do not want him to be killed by the Ingraz. Find him and kill him.'

So, finally, it was said.

The boy let out the breath he had been holding during the last part of the speech. The old man was looking fierce enough to start another ordeal of hot fat at any moment. The legends said that when the hero Shiluti was organising the Great First Raid of the Ao, he threw pieces of hot pork into a blazing fire. His warriors, one by one, picked up the fat and popped it inside their mouth, volunteering to go with him.

Shilukaba didn't have to do that, though. All the young Nagas there were going. It had been decided long before the council.

'I have talked with the elders. There are a few more men who will be going with you. They wait at Mokokchung. You will start from here, but avoid Amguri because we do not want the Ingraz to know. They have not even given us good weapons to fight the Japani. They do not want us to do anything on our own, so they must not know about this, they must not even suspect. You will wear khaki shorts and shirts like our scouts wear. The rest of the men will meet you on the Mokokchung Road. Your weapons, food and water will be with them. From there, you will avoid all the known trails where there is a chance of meeting Ingraz. Avoid their armies at all cost. You will bypass Dimapur ...'

'Suppose the Colonel is at Dimapur?' Gojen asked, now fully involved in the plan.

'There are no senior Japani officers at Dimapur, our men

have found out,' said one of the Aos.

'The Japani are concentrated at Kohima, because they have not captured it completely. You say this Japani is a planner, a schemer. They will most likely use him in Kohima. Not even Imphal. They have already captured Imphal. No, I'm sure this man is at Kohima,' Shilukaba said.

'But you can't be that certain,' KC objected.

'Look at the time. He was at our village on 18 March. The Japani were at Kohima soon after. It is closer. Surely he went there, or was ordered there. Kohima it shall be.'

They had no way of making sure. But that Angami town in the south was their best bet.

'You will have no problems travelling there, unless you find Japani groups. You will have to decide whether to fight them or not. The important thing is to find this man. The Ingraz want to fight the Japani, let them fight on their own.'

'And if we find him, but it is difficult to get to him. What then?' someone asked.

Shilukaba considered this. 'It is possible, but not likely, that he is captured by the Ingraz before you find him. They say the Japani do not surrender easily, so this might not happen. If it does, you will have to find a way of getting to him without the Ingraz finding out.'

'What about the Indians who are fighting with them?'

'There are not many of them with the Japani in the hills yet. Anyway, if they think such people will help them after the Ingraz are defeated ... but it is not our concern. Leave them alone.'

'And once we get him, do we bring you his head?'

It was a reasonable question for the tribe. The Ao had, after all, been headhunters before the British and Christianity stopped the practice after 1889 when the tribe came under the Empire. The taking of heads was a mark of conquest in combat, the heads preserved and displayed in the villages as trophies of victory. Some of the heads were also decorated. There had been special tattoos, circles on the back of the warrior to mark that he had taken heads.

But the old chief shook his head.

'What do you know about taking heads? Even your fathers had not been born then. That was the old way. That was different. We have no need for that now. Besides, we do not want the Ingraz to suspect any Naga tribe of working under their noses. No.'

He leaned over the table and stabbed the photograph with his forefinger.

'He might or might not value his head. We know he values *this*. Bring it.'

5

Oil. It had always been about oil. That part he could understand. But all this was madness he had given up trying to grasp.

Lt General Kotoku Sato, commander, 31st Division, Imperial Japanese Army, was a career soldier. A soldier's soldier who had seen action and risen through the ranks on the first premise that his primary duty lay with the safety of the men he commanded and his second lay in carrying out the mission. Throwing them into the firing line on a whim was not a tactic he supported, whatever the situation.

When the invasion of India, codenamed the U-Go Plan, was being formed, the objective had been simple: a spoiling attack against the IV Corps of the British Indian Army at Imphal. Why did they need to attack the IV Corps? Two reasons: the airfields on the plains of Assam were being used by British and American aircraft to supply food, guns and medical aid to the Chinese partisans under Chiang Kai-Shek. Those airfields needed to be captured to choke off the Chinese resistance, which had stubbornly refused to surrender.

The second reason: to stop the British from recapturing Burma. Why did the Japanese need Burma, specially its northern parts? For its oilfields and mineral reserves. These oil reserves were part of a vast subterranean reservoir extending into eastern Assam, another area which could be held, if feasible. This was the doctrine behind the U-Go Plan. Secure the oil sources and make sure the British do not retake Burma. It was understood. If oil was becoming more and more important in peace, it was doubly so in war.

Into this, Sato mused bitterly, had stepped in the overarching ambition of that blockhead, his superior, Lt General Renya Mutaguchi, commanding officer of the IJA's 15th Army, of which the 31st Division was a part. Mutaguchi had enlarged the plan and converted it into a penetration of India, perhaps even to overthrow the Raj. It was a ridiculous notion at best, thought Lt General Sato: the IJA was already stretched and committed on several fronts, from the Pacific (where the Americans were progressing steadily inwards) to Singapore and Burma. Frontline troops were nearing the limits of their endurance and reserve forces were being chewed up everywhere.

Outwardly, these changes had been kicked around within the army high command before Prime Minister Hideki Tojo shot it down.

In secret, Tojo had given his complete approval, because it appealed to his grand notions about himself. Mutaguchi had drawn up a plan, whose details had never been entirely revealed to Sato, and entrusted its oversight on-field to this madman in front of Sato now: Colonel Shunroku Mori. This was not surprising, considering how the army fed on the connections of a few fortunate officers. Everyone knew that Mori was friends with all the right people. But that did not gloss the fact that Mori was little more than a bully and hardly a soldier. In fact, Sato reminded himself again as he did each time they faced off: this man was a maniac.

One evening at division headquarters in some nameless valley in Burma, shortly before the advance into India, Sato had been voicing his misgivings on his general's plans. It was no secret in the unit that Mutaguchi and he had been in two opposing camps during a bitter feud within the officer corps in the early 1930s. Each faction distrusted the other. But Sato's men trusted him as good soldiers trust good officers.

He had been saying: 'Naturally, we will do well in India. But meanwhile, don't be surprised if we all starve to death because of that idiot Mutaguchi.' His officers had laughed grimly at that.

That evening, Colonel Mori had made his first appearance at divisional headquarters, perhaps descended from the heavens to give lowly creatures like Sato the benefit of his intellect. Sato had seen him occasionally before: a shadowy figure at the ears of senior commanders, advising, whispering, with vaguely derisive looks at the field officers. Sato had never expected him taking over his command. After all, the man was only a *colonel*, wasn't he?

Mori had arrived carrying a direct order from 15th Army headquarters: he was to look into every aspect of the operations and give directions accordingly. He would not be contradicted and would report ultimately to Mutaguchi. Sato had retired to his corner, effectively demoted from actual command.

Along their march from Burma, Sato could only clamp down on his helpless fury as Colonel Mori overrode every decision of the commanders, occasionally disappearing from command posts to make individual forays with his personal unit into the jungles. The more he got to know the man, the more Sato disliked him, with his affectations, that gaudy long knife he carried, his utter unconcern for the enlisted men under him, his complete inability to understand the realities of war. So he thought he could plan out and win a campaign, did he? Any private could have told him that battles never go where the plan tells them to go. Battles are their own masters.

Sato knew the man was a psychopath and must not be left unsupervised. Ironically, such a man held the keys to the campaign.

And here they were, with other senior commanders, in 31st Division's field headquarters at Kohima. If they had expected to take Kohima Ridge in an overwhelming attack, they had been wrong. Sato hoped they would some day be right, for once.

'... And it was all your fault,' Colonel Mori was directing the transferred ire of 15th Army high command on Lt Gen Miyazaki. It was unbelievable, thought Sato, watching the exchange. Miyazaki was a brilliant soldier and commander. He had defeated the British Parachute Brigade near Imphal. What was the Japanese soldier expected to do when he met the British, turn and run? So that was the new doctrine now, was it?

Miyazaki would not let it pass.

'The British brigade was in our direct line of advance. It had to be destroyed. I did not see an alternative. Headquarters surely understands that,' he said.

'Fighting for six days with a brigade? It slowed your advance to this town. It delayed you. Your group could have taken this town before our other elements reached here. You gave the British more time!' Mori was nearly shouting now.

Sato thought there was a simpler reason for Mori's anger: he was jealous of more able commanders.

'Our situation here could be improved now. We are progressing well. It is the advance line to the west I am worried about. The high command should release more elements for Dimapur,' Sato intervened, asking Mori. *Every* request had to go through the idiot.

'Our men are disciplined. Morale is high. Dimapur is in our hands. We will advance from there into the plains,' Mori said, repeating his pet phrase.

'Morale will not prevail against artillery and air support, *Rikugun-san*. Even as we speak, the British 161st Infantry Brigade is flying down to Dimapur. Intelligence says they have an artillery regiment with them. If that is true, our men at Dimapur will be outmatched. We cannot progress further if we get tied down at every town we encircle.'

It had not always been like this. When the Japanese Army reached Dimapur, there had been virtually no defenders to stop them. But Mori had stalled. Mori had sent messages back and forth with headquarters and declared the objective was to occupy Dimapur and consolidate. Now the British were rushing reinforcements to that front. The element of surprise and superiority was vanishing.

'We will concentrate on getting rid of the defenders here. Then we will advance in full strength into the plains. The British will never have enough forces to recapture Dimapur before we are ready.'

Kohima had been another headache. The small unit of the British Indian Army defending the headquarters of the Naga Hills district had fought the Japanese for every inch of the hillsides. The hill the Japanese Army had come to refer to as *Inu* Hill (*dog*, how appropriate), which the British called Garrison Hill, had repelled wave after wave of the invaders. Casualties were mounting.

'We can encircle them and advance for now. We can always capture the defences here later. The high command must be notified that we must advance to the other side of the hills,' Sato tried again. Did they not know that it was easier to repel the British if they fought from the heights and the British were stranded on the plains?

'*Must?* The high command does not like being ordered by field commanders, General,' Mori warned. 'They have decided, and I agree, that we are to concentrate our attack on Kohima. The British will never be able to send in enough reinforcements before we reach the plains.'

'They have air support. They have bombers and transport aircraft. Where are our aircraft?' Miyazaki cut in.

Naturally, there were few. Those in Burma were needed to battle the RAF's sorties. More aircraft could not be flown in, with the losses in the Pacific.

'I want you to pass on to high command that I follow their directive with reluctance. I still say we must advance now and not give the British time,' Sato said, got up heavily and left with the commanders.

Colonel Shunroku Mori watched them go, pitying their inability to understand. But then, all through his life, he had never been understood by those around him.

He had been the second son of a tax inspector in Osaka. It was a government job, but did not pay much, nor was the work like in western countries. There was no respect either, for his father would go knocking from door to door with reports and calculations in hand and ask for payment of taxes. People respected the Emperor very much but not the nondescript representative in shabby western clothes at their door who wanted their money.

Shunroku was the second son. Everyone liked his elder brother: a bright, clever boy, a favourite of the teachers, always excelling at sports and studies, even at calligraphy, where his work with the alphabet was held up as an example to the whole school. Shunroku, in contrast, had been slow to learn things. His classmates would make fun of him. He used to rage at his helplessness, his slow wit. He was not helpless now, was he?

His brother, who he hated with a deep, passionate black hate, would try to help. Yes, of course. It was another way of saying: I am better than you, I am your crutch, Mori thought. The bullying, taunts and beatings at school only meant he became a worse student.

Things improved for him after his brother left for Tokyo to study law. No longer overshadowed, he worked hard at his studies and passed his exams. But he could only get minor government clerking jobs until he joined the Army War College at Shiroya. And he had only done that because studies were free there.

He kept his rage at the world carefully hidden, nursing his envy of his more able college mates. He worked hard at the physical tests and later during training, although he had known that here, too, he would not be superlative. He made friends among his classmates selectively, choosing those he saw were likely to advance. Among them was his junior, Masanobu Tsuji.

He found Tsuji a similar soul, full of rage and hatred, but masked by a smiling, joking exterior, always ready with witty remarks, always well-groomed and popular with certain types of people, mainly the fanatics and the self-styled empire-builders.

They had each identified the other's boiling distrust for those around them. Together they would talk about the society they saw around them, and what they would do, given a chance. They had both considered their future careers in the Army as a personal journey and not really as work they would be doing for the country.

One evening, they had been drinking at an officers' bar

in Tokyo, talking about this officer or that, and what fools most people were. Tsuji got increasingly angry at his life and his past and the laughing, happy people around him.

They had walked out and gone to the back, where they got wood and kindling and set fire to the rear exit and the first floor.

The bar had burnt down.

Mori and Tsuji had stood across the street from the front entrance, watching and smiling in their hearts, watching their fellow officers staggering out in the smoke and flames, many of them injured. Tsuji had drunkenly shouted that some day the whole spoilt establishment would burn like this. Tsuji had been noticed because he had shouted. Mori had kept quiet.

Now Tsuji was a powerful officer too, based in China. They had both advanced on their connections and friends in high places. Both had many awards to boast of, including the Order of the Sacred Treasure (3rd Class) and the Order of the Rising Sun (4th Class). And now he had a Colonel's star too, didn't he?

Fighting and dying in a hole somewhere, the Colonel reflected, gathering up his papers, was for those who did not understand the true meaning of being an officer. An officer leads. An officer commands. An officer is not a tax inspector walking the streets. He was not like his elder brother either, the handsome young man who gave up law and joined the Navy and died in a cruiser at the Battle of Bismarck Sea the year before.

No. He was a leader who ordered men; who was obeyed.

Good taste. That was another thing about him too. His fellow officers carried factory-made *shin-gunto*, mass-produced katana swords, as part of their ceremonial wear. It was a nod to the older days, but for all that, it was an empty gesture.

71

Swords in the hands of the great *bushi* had been works of art, a matter of personal choice, lovingly created by master craftsmen. Each part of the sword had a specialist to build it. An officer's *shin-gunto* today was like any other, just as drab and tasteless, just another cutting instrument. As if commanders were produced in a factory somewhere. As if everything was supposed to be functional, that was all.

No. He would not carry that cheap piece of metal. In its place (by special arrangement) he had a companion sword, a shorter *katana* called a *wakizashi* with beautiful engravings on its hilt and scabbard, a gift from Tsuji nearly ten years earlier. The last time they had met, more than a year and a half ago, Tsuji had been preparing to leave for an island called Guadalcanal, where he had (doubtless) fought heroically against Americans.

The sword was a genuine piece of craftsmanship, though he did not know how old it was. It was exquisitely beautiful and, he was sure, envied by his fellow officers.

Look at me, he thought, tying the *wakizashi* to his belt and leaving divisional command headquarters for his personal observation post. Where are all those boys who used to make fun of stupid little Shunroku? Where are they now? Where is my clever elder brother? Look at me today: I am a soldier and commander, and I have a beautiful sword to prove it.

*

'He might or might not value his head. The Ingraz say he has never been seen without his long knife. So, he values it. Kill him and bring it to me,' said an old Ao chief, stabbing at the photograph in front of him on a small wooden table in the study of a house on a tea estate on the plains of Assam.

6

It was only a basic plan, so naturally they had to talk some more about the finer details.

There would be ponies, of course. With the weapons and food and the need to travel swiftly over the hills, the men would be slowed down unless they had pack animals. For the greater part of the journey, anyway.

Half a dozen more men would join them on the Mokokchung Road. All the Aos working as scouts with the British had been told what had happened. There would be more men wherever they went.

What about the other tribes? Gojen wanted to ask, but this was a sensitive matter. The tribes had been trying to work together for some time, but there were always issues of protocol and violent history to be worked through. Certainly, he thought, the other tribes knew about the massacre. But he could not tell if anything would follow from this.

Clothes. When the war broke into the Naga Hills, the tribesmen had volunteered with the British Army. They had been named the Naga Scouts and given uniforms: khaki shorts and shirts. Most went barefoot as they were accustomed to. They had also been armed with muskets. The British had been quick to realise that the tribesmen were the best in tracking Japanese in the hills. These were their hills, after all.

The finer points were raised at the council. Most problems had been solved. It was not possible, everyone said, to get accurate, immediate information about the fighting. But there were runners in the hills, most working in the British lines, and they had been told to bring information along the trails as often as they could. The British would not notice occasional absent 'native' faces.

Gojen watched all this from the sidelines. KC said his information from the British in Calcutta was very good, very detailed. He had done a good job. He had given them a lot of data to go ahead with, including the photograph, which everyone thought could not have been clearer. The boy was happy to have been of use.

A small voice somewhere asked him if he had done enough. He had hardly *done* anything, had he really?

He leaned over the wooden rails of the balcony running around the first floor of the house in the afternoon. It was getting warmer. The rains might begin soon.

It was a large house with high ceilings, airy. The pillars were of good wood. The first floor and the stairs were also of wood. The walls on the ground floor were of brick up to two feet, after which they were of *ikora*, elephant grass found in some variety across the valley. Shelter and food for the rhino, elephant grass is thick and strong when dried, but light too, making it a safe building tool. In the event of an earthquake, dry grass falling on someone's head tends to hurt less than a clay brick.

The dry grass was plastered over with mud, finished smooth and painted, the wall bisected at intervals by supports of wood. The ceilings were also of wood panels. The windows were quarter panes of glass which weren't

74

cleaned as often as they should have been. Wooden furniture, comfortable cane chairs, comfortable beds to sleep in, soft pillows to rest his head. It was a *happy* house, a *peaceful* house. He was to stay.

All the bedrooms were on the first floor, covered by a sloping tin roof. He was looking down on one end of the veranda next to KC's study downstairs, watching two of the Nagas and the Konyak in the courtyard, talking. That is, the Nagas were talking and the Konyak was silent. Gojen wondered what he must have been through, what he thought about behind the blank stare.

They would leave shortly. Tonight, it appeared. They would want to get deep inside the hills without meeting any of the plainsmen they knew.

What could he do now? He had gone out after the council, waited for Meren to finish and collared him for a while. Then he had gone walking around, finally reaching the estate's processing plant. He had spent a few hours in the garage with bunches of paper and a knife. Now he was just asking himself: they will start soon on the road to a place where they didn't know what would happen at all. What can I do?

'You could at least try to look less worried.' KC had come up the stairs and was trying to guess his mood, as usual. He was stuffing his pipe, still trying to make the most of a temporary vacation from marriage.

'I don't look worried.'

'But you are. You want to go with them.'

'I don't know if it will work.'

'The plan? We don't know enough to say definitely what will happen to them. They have all the things they need. Getting more men won't be a problem. The only thing they need to look out for is the British.'

The boy just nodded and looked across the estate spread out beneath them.

'You know you can't go with them. Not even to where the hills begin.'

'I am not thinking about it at all.'

'This is not some wild prank you boys used to do in their village. This is much, much bigger. You can't even begin to understand.'

'What is it?'

'It is a very cruel place. I don't want to talk about it. The men know what they are going into. You did your work. Now we all stay here and wait for news.'

'The runners will come here?'

'It has all been arranged. We will hear from them if anything big happens.'

'But it will take time.'

KC leaned over the rails as well.

'It will take a little time,' he admitted. 'But at least we will know if they find him. Shouldn't you be doing something, instead of brooding? Aren't you going to the range?'

'I don't want to, right now.'

KC was shocked. This had *never* happened before. He narrowed his eyes.

'Have you damaged the rifle?' he asked suspiciously.

'No, of course not. It is in my room. I just don't want to do anything till they leave.'

Now the Ao chief and Meren were talking about something or the other.

The boy straightened up and walked to the stairs.

'Can I read a book in your study?'

'I thought you said you didn't want to do anything.'

'I just want to look at some books.'

'Which ones?'

'I don't know. Anything, I think.'
'Go on. But don't damage them with your big hands.'

*

It never ceased to amaze Lt Col. Kenneally of His Majesty's Intelligence Corps that a small group of fierce men could cause so much damage in such a short amount of fighting. Dimapur was in flames.

He had arrived on 15 April by a very uncomfortable transport plane packed with troops and guns from Calcutta. They had landed on a makeshift strip in a meadow near the town, the sound of artillery and small arms in the distance. The plains were full of trucks, mules and ponies. It was Uncle Bill's idea.

Colonel William Slim had been asked to take command of the British Burma offensive. Slim was from the British Indian Army and at the moment held a wartime rank of Major General and the temporary rank of Lt General. He was a Military Cross winner from the earlier War, had fought the Germans in Africa and was as cunning a commander as he was popular with the troops. Therefore, Uncle Bill.

Slim had taken one long look at the terrain and quickly agreed with his officers that transport held the keys to the Burma campaign. If the army was to be regularly supplied over the hills and ravines and muddy tracks that passed for roads in this part of the world, he said, they would have to use pack animals where vehicles could not pass. The idea was beginning to make a difference.

Kenneally met other officers of his unit near the airstrip. He was to prepare a briefing for Uncle Bill.

The British Army and the British Indian Army had both been surprised by the suddenness and scale of the invasion. It had long been thought that the Japanese advance would stop in Burma. No indications had surfaced of any designs on India itself. With the Japanese tied up with the Allies in rearguard fighting in Burma, and their losses in the Pacific, the idea that they would push even more westward had been unthinkable. As always, the unthinkable had happened and the front now stretched more than sixty miles across difficult hill terrain, from the plains town of Dimapur, deep into the Imphal valley to the south.

The British had been caught napping but were desperately trying to catch up and now the news that Kenneally received was good.

Many events had happened in the early days of the fighting, but the most remarkable of these were, of course, also the most unexpected. In the first week of April, with the Japanese spearhead reaching Kohima, the British 161st Brigade, which had retreated west, was ordered forward again, into the thick of the enemy's advance. The idea then had been to slow down the Japanese. But to everyone's disbelief, a battalion from this brigade—The Queen's Own Royal West Kent Regiment—had advanced *through* the Japanese lines and reached Kohima, where they joined the defenders for the remainder of the siege.

The British 2nd Division, the unit Kenneally had mentioned to Rev Bartlett as doing an amphibian invasion rehearsal in southern India, had started arriving in Dimapur early in April. By the eleventh of that month, the British 14th Army finally had as many men over the front as the invaders had brought in.

Meanwhile, the fighting around the plains of Dimapur was hard, with the Japanese contesting the British from house to house, ridge to ridge. Most of the town and neighbouring villages had been destroyed in the shelling, the broken thatch and tin houses somehow still standing, the local residents all fled before the invaders. But the Japanese held their ground, British reinforcements and bombings or not, and were in no mood to give up. That was not new.

The Intelligence officer was informed that the 5th Brigade of their 2nd Division had broken through the Japanese lines that morning to a small town in the Angami hills, called Jotsoma, two miles from Kohima, rescuing the 161st Brigade whose men, in army terms, were getting 'cooked' in a siege. 161st Brigade, despite the siege, had been providing some artillery support to the garrison in Kohima, but they were running short of water, ammunition and men.

'That relieves …' the Lt Col. concluded, looking over the field maps in a small tent with the roar of gunfire and vehicles outside, '161st Brigade to direct their attention to Kohima. That is a distance of five miles over the roads. These distances do add up in the hills, don't they? This road goes over more than twice the direct distance from Jotsoma to Kohima. Do we have any accurate information on Japanese movement from Kohima?'

'They have dug in on hill spurs, the RAF says, with mortar and some mobile artillery pieces. But there is no mass troop movement from Kohima towards here,' a Major reported.

'Hmm. So they are not advancing. I wonder why. If we were in their place, would we not press forward as quickly as we could?'

'The RAF confirms most of the soldiers are still laying siege to Kohima.'

'In that case, we should rush through the break in their lines as soon as we can. 161st Brigade it is, then. Can they have artillery and air support from other elements?'

The RAF representative said yes, they could bomb

Japanese positions up to Kohima. They had been doing that all along, hadn't they? But they could not drop bombs on Kohima itself because British and Japanese fighters were too near each other there.

'Fine. I will take this recommendation to the General. 161st Brigade to push through to our boys in Kohima, God bless them. You know, I think the General will be very pleased with the progress.'

For General Slim had arrived in Dimapur.

*

He stood, leaning against a pillar on the veranda. The men were preparing to leave.

Their chief was at the steps of the house, having a final word with them. They were all in scout uniform, tarpaulin satchels across their backs. They would make it. They would walk through the night, reaching the Mokokchung Road, and then onward till they met the rest of the men with their weapons, food and other items. It was beginning.

KC came away from the group and stood by his grandson.

'You don't have anything to say to them, as a goodbye?'

'I talked with Meren.'

'They are ready. They might even have a chance.'

He looked at KC. 'You really think so? With so many men and so much fighting, do you think they can find one man and reach him?'

'They will not be found by the British, at least. Maybe they will be lucky.'

The boy didn't say anything to that.

'You haven't said a word about wanting to go. You want to go with them, don't you?'

'I don't have to say anything,' he said, his voice even, blank.

'You can't fool your grandfather, boy. I know everything about you. I can see your heart ...'

'*Koka*, you don't have to start talking like that now ...'

'You want to go with them. You want to help them. You want to be in this thing.'

The boy didn't say anything.

'You can't go, you know.'

He looked at KC then, in the eye, straight and level, not blinking.

'I can't go. I know that.'

KC lied. He could not see into the boy's heart, if at all anyone could. He looked at the black, flat, emotionless eyes of his grandson in the gathering evening. He tried to find something, a trace of feeling, helplessness, even anger or sadness or misery or grief.

He found just a blank stare.

Where had this boy come from? KC asked himself. Why was he so different from KC's sons and grandsons, brothers and nephews and nieces? Where had he learnt this odd *stillness*? Where had he learnt to stare like that? Why couldn't KC get any idea what the boy was thinking about? Who was this boy?

They had dinner in the evening, the two old men and Gojen. It was a good dinner with fish, and the boy ate well, KC observed. That was a good sign, wasn't it? They would wait for news, and meanwhile, he thought, he would spend more time with his grandson, talk to him, go with him to the range.

They went to bed at about ten-thirty: in all matters, people here began the day early and ended it early. KC and his friend did not sleep.

At midnight, they crept down the passage and opened the

door to the boy's room. He was sleeping with heavy dreams.

'I did not think it would be so easy with him,' KC said in relief as they closed the door and went back.

'He didn't ask me to send him with them. Did he ask you?' the Naga chief whispered.

'Not a word. He just didn't say anything.'

They could not explain it.

At two in the morning, the boy opened the door to the outer passage, climbed over the railing and down a pillar.

7

'What are these?'

Gojen, thirteen, stood near Fuller's desk in his study, during one of their numerous talks on firearms. He held three live rounds in his palm. They were the same size and looked the same type as his rifle bullets, except their tips had been hollowed, forming concave indents. They spoke a different language.

'Oh, those? I'm afraid they are of little use to you, lad,' Fuller said, taking one out of a cardboard box and rolling it between his thumb and forefinger.

'They are a different kind of bullet. Better, or worse, depends on how you look at it. Not for marksmanship. Not even for hunting, actually, though I have seen a few … men, use them so.'

And, of course, the boy had to know everything about them.

'When someone decides to write the full and final book on the great rifles of the world, these bullets will be India's single biggest claim to fame, in a very twisted way. The story goes back to when the British Indian Army was fighting in Afghanistan. You've read about the Afghan Wars, of course?'

Gojen had heard some parts of it.

'They are tough fighters, the tribes in those mountains. Rather straightforward folk, like your friends, but easier to provoke and more experienced, if you look at history. Everyone, from Alexander to us, has been crossing Afghanistan through the ages, you know, threshold to India and all that, and the Afghans have been fighting right down the line. Damn difficult to stop an Afghan coming at you, even if he has a rusty old sword from his grandfather's third cousin and you have a Martini-Henry, like the British troops had. Frighten whole bunches of men right about turn and march double-quick back to India.' Fuller chuckled at the thought a little.

'So, after the Tommies did a bit of the fighting and got a taste of Afghan hospitality, someone probably thought: we need something else to stop them. Now, those bullets you use, they're Spitzers, right?'

Gojen said yes, and it sounded German to him.

'Well, so that bright someone took a cartridge, not unlike yours, and made those cones on the tip. Now, with a tip, as you know, the bullet goes right into the target, and if it is fast and heavy enough, comes out the other side and makes a hole the same size as when it enters. But with the tip gone ...' He leaned forward and spoke slowly. 'A larger part of the bullet strikes the target. You see how it works, don't you? The larger the part, the more tissue inside the body it affects, and if it comes out, it tears off a hole as big as this.' He bunched his large hand into a fist. 'Ugly business, mind you, very ugly. That's why I said it is not for hunters.'

'Did it work?'

'For the Tommies, you mean? In a way, but you don't win a war like that by inventing a bullet, there are other things involved and ... anyway, it became popular. British armies used it in Africa, those Boers used it against us, Americans used it against natives, everyone having a merry time.

'And then comes the comical part. Pretty soon there was fighting in Europe, as always, and then everyone said: wait a while, you can't use *those* bullets here. I mean, we are all civilised people, you can't use bullets you use against savages, so let us shoot at each other with these nice pointy bullets, like before. All those civilised countries met at the Hague in Holland ...'

The Hague, Holland, went the boy's mind, clicking on the pieces of information.

'... and signed a treaty in 1899 which does not allow these bullets to be used by soldiers of those countries. Ha. There you go. Meanwhile, people have been experimenting, so now you have different varieties. Some with a bit of cellulose, you know, it's a type of hard paper, in the middle, so the bullet breaks on impact. Other bullets have some soft metal on the cone. I keep them for the variety, never used one. And here endeth today's lesson. Run down to your house if you want your grandmother to let me visit KC later, will you?'

At the door Gojen, a little wiser, asked, 'What are they called, Fuller, sir?'

'You have seen the aerodrome near your school?' He pronounced it as *aye-row*.

'Yes...'

'So there used to be a big arsenal there back then. These little monsters are all home-grown: that's where they were invented. So they are called after the arsenal. Dum-Dums.'

8

But he had never returned those three rounds.

These were now wrapped singly in a new kind of shiny paper the estate had begun using to coat the insides of tea crates. They were supposed to keep the damp from the leaves while shipping them out over land and sea. He reasoned they could keep the leaves from the brass rounds too. Fifty more of his usual cartridges were wrapped likewise. The truth was, he did not know how many might be enough. The rounds were pushed deep inside a small box of fresh tea leaves and slung on the handle of an old Raleigh bicycle that had been lying in a corner of the truck garage and no one had remembered. He had.

The rifle's size had been a problem: its three feet and eight inches would be difficult to hide, and for this phase, hiding was the key. The solution was a long piece of bamboo, its divisions inside hollowed over a few hours' work, lined with strips of the shiny paper. The rifle was wrapped, placed inside and stoppered at the other end with a coating of paper and mud.

The problem *this* ingenuity caused was weight: the rifle weighed nearly eight pounds to begin with. The bamboo, being a thick-stemmed *bholuka*, was heavy. The combined weight meant it had to be strung on the horizontal bar beneath the seat, where it brushed his ankles as he pedalled.

Still, it served his purpose. He was wearing khaki shorts, the oldest shirt he could find with a few buttons missing, tennis shoes (caked with mud to look older than they were) around the handlebar, socks hidden among the springs under the seat. With his hair ruffled and a little greasy, he now looked like the numerous errand boys in the plantations who combined several duties: selling fish, country-made *lau-pani*, samples of tea at the big houses. The tea box was to look like a tea box, the bamboo a vat where the finest vintage day-old country liquor was fermented and sold in.

The deception was necessary along the route he was now pedalling in the hours before dawn. The war's inching nearer had meant the administration now put policemen on patrol over the back roads near where the Naga Hills began, a wild, forested area where news of any disturbance brought out dacoits and brigands to take advantage of the law's weaknesses. The policemen were also there to make sure civilians did not mistakenly journey into the hills in wartime as freely as before and to direct the movement of armed Nagas coming the opposite way.

These were the famed red-turbanned *ronga* police, also in khaki shorts, impressive, and in a way liked by the villagers. They were mostly local men who usually, unless pushed by their superiors, looked the other way during independence demonstrations. But they were a suspicious species and the rifle, of course, had to be hidden.

He pedalled on through the night, occasionally pulling on the steel-pipe brakes of the ancient cycle. The tattered seat under him was a little uncomfortable, the springs under the seat thick, rusted and hard. The front and rear mudguards were barely attached to the frame, rattling as he went over the pebbles, the right pedal dangling on its hinges. The roads on this stretch, as indeed everywhere, were pebbled clearances. They made for good walking, but were bumpy to ride on. The new dynamo from the Anglo's shop powered a small electric bulb to give a wavering light out in front; the faster he pedalled, the stronger the light, but he had a long distance to go and must not tire himself out in a sprint.

A cat, or maybe a mongoose, streaked across the road just beyond the light, escaping from the grounds of one estate to another. The forests and small creeks between and around the estates and villages had all kinds of wild animals: small foxes and jackals, squirrels and monkeys, a few pygmy hogs, civets, even the occasional leopard. The predators sometimes raided villages for chickens or small goats, the villagers and estates workers in their shanty huts ever on the lookout for them with bow and arrow, axe and stick. And the big families, those who could afford it, had guns. But by far the biggest menace were elephants.

These small forest patches were connected or separated by small distances, forming an arc of sorts that led along the base of the Naga Hills westward into Golaghat and the Reserve, as Kaziranga was now commonly called. Begun as a British experiment at conservation—after several decades of rather indiscriminate hunts up and down both banks of the Brahmaputra—animals were now protected, within the Reserve. The problem with this was, the animals didn't know their special status was limited to Kaziranga, so they tried to roam as they had done before.

Where the forests had been cut down for estates or farms, animals, crossing from one green patch to the next, collided with man. Large herds of wild elephants were frequently sighted near villages and estates, which if unlucky were invaded and trampled: banana, plantain and rice husks were ransacked, thatch huts were brushed aside and general anarchy prevailed. Planters, as often as not, gathered reputation duelling with these rampaging herds, .50 calibre 'elephant guns' were brought out and brandished, and life went on. Single tuskers were more frequent, their rampages equally deadly, and travel along roads at night was not advisable.

Gojen wondered, as he heard a fox whine somewhere across the tea shrubs, what he would do if he came across a tusker. There had been no reports of any here, but you could never be sure. There was not much he could do against a leopard either—although these were very shy—with an unloaded rifle inside a hollow bamboo.

Down the pebbly lanes, up and down inclines he had to watch out in case he fell and broke something. Past groves of betel, palm and coconut, bamboo and banana, thick underbrush, cicadas croaking out their fortnight's existences.

Meren's group had a seven hours' start, but on foot. They were to travel east, seventeen miles to … which reminded the boy of another minor headache. Bartlett and his maths teacher had gone to some lengths to explain to the boys that the new metric system was here to stay. India had converted to it—at least on paper—four years earlier, although Britain hadn't yet. The British students at the school—the wittier ones—had quipped that a 'French' system of weights and measures would never hold, but anyhow, Gojen had to go through several conversion tables and had been told to think with the metric system. How many grains made a gram (16.4 and on and on), how many centimetres to an inch (twelve inches to thirty centimetres), how many kilometres to a mile (1.6) and metres to a yard (they were nearly equal, thankfully). This new system was so complicated, he thought. It was bad enough re-calculating distances he had known all his life; it was worse estimating distances in his head *and* converting, in which he never got it right at once. If yards and miles had been good enough so far, that is how they should stay.

Seventeen miles east to Amguri, across a small river. Amguri was the last big plainstown before the hills began, a regular trading post of old, the road going up towards Mokokchung in Ao land, and beyond.

But Meren and his companions were all known at Amguri, so they would head southward before they reached the river, climbing into the hills much west of the road even if it made difficult going. Once there, they would walk deeper into the hills before reaching Mokokchung Road.

He would parallel the route, his mind working out their approximate positions at the moment. Meren would make them walk briskly to avoid the *ronga* police if possible. Once they entered the hills, it was easier to travel without meeting anyone, specially in these times with the tribes moving out and the villages empty.

Mokokchung would not be empty, though. Mokokchung, deep in Ao land, the citadel of the northern Aos for ages, the village established, some claimed, by the great Shiluti himself. It had seen the great days of the rise of the Aos and their expansion northward into the plains, the tribe spreading north and east, even across the Luit to the lands of the Adi. There was a Baptist church there now, and a pastor, but the crossbow and the spear were there too. The people had stayed and would stay on, just as some of the Keuhimiyas of Kohima had not left. Some of the young men had joined up as scouts for the British; some others had simply vanished with a quiet word or two. Gojen had an idea these latter were in the forests doing what Meren and his men were to do.

Gojen would take a different network of lanes, moving closer southward. It would mean cycling nearly thirty miles and then some walking on foot, which he wanted to avoid for as long as possible, because of the bamboo. But sooner or later he would have to climb up and catch them at a bend along the trail he had in mind. His only prayer was: please, make the elephants go away.

An occasional dog would bark at him as he rode on, the night got colder, even the foxes went to sleep, with dawn just around. He estimated he had made half his journey by now, which meant about fifteen miles, which in kilometres meant fifteen multiplied by this and divided by that and … forget it.

Chnk.

He stopped pedalling and the chain made a whizzing noise but stayed tight; it hadn't come off. That would delay him some more. A puncture would mean it was over, unless he stole another bicycle, which he wasn't sure he could do. He would decide if it happened. Anyhow, bicycles were rare too, weren't they? A villager would probably pull his inside the hut and tie it to his bed, he supposed. He had seen a few who did.

These villages were familiar to him even if only vague outlines could be seen. He remembered practically each lane, pond and creek in this area. Some parts of the hills were also familiar. Beyond, who knew?

Turning down a lane and taking another, the lamplight steadier now, his legs in rhythm. A sort of glow from somewhere to his left, beyond a banana grove. It was coming to morning. He could see the outlines of the hills now, towering up in the distance. He bent over the handlebars. Let us push a bit and see.

Around a bend, the outline of a single figure, walking, his back towards the rider. Not bright enough to see if … yes, a red turban. The mudguards rattled on cue, the *ronga* police turned, stick in hand.

'*Oi! Ro! Rokh!*' Stop. And if you don't stop, I will chase you, cycle or not and catch you, for you must be up to something. A good policeman always suspects; it becomes his nature. Presumably he does not feel good until he has suspected at least once in the morning.

Gojen slowed down, pulling up the brakes. The policeman came up, looked at him up and down and at the bicycle. Gojen put on the hangdog expression of a hard-working simpleton.

'From?'

'Nijora, *saar*.' A village he remembered passing some distance behind.

'*Koloi jao?*' The accent suggested a local, so he had to be very careful telling him where he was going, to whom and so on. Everyone knew everyone here.

'Amguri.'

'You could have gone in the other direction and taken the lane to the river. It is shorter.'

'*O*,' said the boy, with a look suggesting the idea of cutting travel time and work would not have occurred to him on its own. 'I always go down this lane.'

'Eh.' The policeman spat and scratched his head, adjusting the turban. 'What is in the box, tea leaves?'

'For the magistrate's house. It is a new kind from a garden …'

'I have met him. I know what the magistrate drinks,' said the policeman importantly, showing off his connections to a lowly villager.

No, you don't. I do, thought the boy. The magistrate was related by marriage.

'And the bamboo, heh? What is it?' He looked it over, noticed the mud cover and smiled a very crooked smile. '*O. O. Ketiya bonua?*' When was it made? Everyone, even those who do not touch it, want to know all about a *lau-pani*'s vintage. It would still take a few days to ferment well: the boy was counting on this to stop the policeman from asking him to break open the seal.

'Yesterday. It is for Bora near the river …' Which was a safe thing to say. There were probably a few hundred men surnamed Bora near the river.

'What, you think I think it is for the magistrate? Heh. *Ja.* Go. That is a very fine cycle—you are lucky you don't have to walk.'

The boy got on and pushed off.

'*Oi!*' Turning back, the policeman, walking up faster. Was something wrong, he thought rapidly. Was the seal on the bamboo, facing the rear, broken? Had the *ronga* idiot seen something resembling a rifle muzzle? Would he ask about the old-new shoes next?

He came close, dropped his voice and said:

'You don't have a knife, do you?'

It was in a pocket in his shorts, a very special knife.

'*Nai, saar.*'

The policeman's smile was almost sheepish. 'I had to cut a betel nut. *Hobo ja.* I will have to bite it, but my teeth are not strong any more.'

He had passed a very minor test, but passed.

Cows were being led out to the fields by the farmers later in the morning, a few stragglers grazing near a stream when he reached the base of the hills. It was a gentler slope here than anywhere nearby. The lane he had been following for the past twenty minutes sloped upwards in a curve from here and he leant over the handles, pushing it up. Very soon the incline became steeper and he got down and pushed. In some village behind and below him, a *naam-ghor*, a community prayer house and cultural centre, opened for the day. Someone began beating the *doba*, a drum nearly as large as a man, in slow, deep and rhythmic beats, accompanying softer cymbals and prayers to Krishna. The drums at this distance drowned out the singers. It was another sound of the plains that petered off as he climbed further. Behind him the plains stretched far north to the Luit, a patchwork emerald blanket of fields and meadows crossed by silver sparkling streams.

It was slow progress from here, but carrying the bamboo on the bicycle meant he could still walk fast. Where the trail curved downhill, he placed a foot on a pedal and scissored faster. Thus he came to Big Stone.

The hills of the region are impossibly green always, giving the impression that these are bottomless mounds of very fertile earth. But deep down inside, their bones are made of hard granite, limestone and other rocks. The Big Stone was one such, a landmark and a common meeting place on Mokokchung Road, tall as ten or twelve men placed one on top of the other, and wide at the base. How deep it went inside the hill on which it stood, nobody knew, and only a small part of it really emerged on the face: a steep mass of granite made smooth by rain.

At the base of Big Stone the boy stopped finally, coming out from under the trees cautiously, eased the bicycle on its side—it did not have a stand either—stretched and considered matters. There was no one to be seen or heard on either end along this stretch. Now to wait. Meren and his men must have made good time, if they hadn't met anyone they knew, and would be coming round the bend in a while.

It was like this that Meren found the boy, sitting on a small stone, his back against the giant rock, eyes half-closed, chewing on a *bon* stalk and looking at a sheaf of loose papers with drawings on them.

'What, maps?'

The boy looked up and inclined his head outward in greeting, his face as impassive as the rest. 'I drew some of them from *koka*'s survey books. Kohima Ridge and the nearby hills. The maps are good, I think, but they don't have much detail.'

'All the surveying was done by the Angami of those hills. Naturally the maps are good. But the Ingraz don't need to know every hill and stone and tree, so they don't put them on the map. They only need to know the villages and the distances. And what you did was very foolish.'

'What?'

Meren took up the leaves of paper, looked at them, sighed and shook his head, and cuffed the boy with the bundle alongside his head. 'You still have much to learn. You are supposed to be an idiot village boy who shouldn't be trusted with the simplest tasks. You go through all this … box and bamboo and whatnot, to avoid questions. How does it look to someone if you sit by the road reading papers? We are not safe until we leave this road. You should have remembered.'

Gojen hadn't thought of that one.

'Anyway, have you learnt anything from them?'

'Only a rough idea. I wanted to bring the maps but *koka* would not like that.'

'Neither of them will like this anyway. Did anyone see you?'

'No, I left when I said I would. No one was awake. They both believed I would not do anything. I thought they wouldn't be sure.'

'Maybe they weren't. Maybe they suspected and still let you decide without telling you.'

'Tch. I don't know. I don't think so. They will have found out by now. Maybe they won't think you had a hand.'

'It does not matter, so long as you follow the rules I told you.'

Gojen pushed the bicycle upright and joined the group, walking further uphill. Meren and he had agreed that the Ao chieftain's general idea needed a lot of refining. For one, events in the hills were moving so swiftly that only a vague outline of a plan of action could be formed. What new situations would emerge was anybody's guess. Finding one man, even a senior officer, among seven thousand Japanese would not be easy.

The boy had told Meren that he had the training and knew a few things about the British which might come in useful, even to the Nagas. But Meren was chiefly concerned with the look he had seen on Gojen's face when he first gave him the news. He did not want to return from whatever way this mission ended and face the unresolved grief within the boy for the rest of his life. Meren wanted him to come along if it made him feel better. Besides, in the eyes of the Naga, the boy was at a man's age.

But Meren had warned him that he could come only if he was under command, not to do anything under his own steam or alone. And he would, at all costs, even of turning back, stay away from the thick of events. Observe, try and figure how this colonel ticked, work on information the Nagas got, make suggestions. The boy had agreed to these terms.

'Did you see anyone on the road?'

'Just a *ronga* policeman. Did you?'

'No one who knew us. Those who saw us will not remark too much on it.'

The boy stopped and looked behind him.

'Do you hear that?'

Meren and the others stopped as well. They heard a while later.

"Convoys. Ingraz."

9

This was going nowhere, fast.

Lt Gen Sato sat down with the feeling that, once again, he had been ramming his head, hard and repeatedly, against a very stubborn brick wall.

'Colonel-*san*,' he said, for though it hurt his pride, he had to be stiffly formal with the man. 'Please let the General understand: the situation is changing. Perhaps it is changing faster than we can control. The British have broken through here ...' he pointed at Jotsoma, 'and practically lifted our siege. But they have not rested there. Even now they push forward uphill. We must be permitted to divert our troops from here to stop the British advance before it gathers momentum, while we still have the advantage.'

The Colonel was patient. The Colonel understood. He had to make these dullards understand the wisdom of headquarters' commands and his analysis of the situation. He spoke slowly, as if explaining to a not-too-bright student, never mind if Sato outranked him.

'General Sato, I have gone over the situation and have informed headquarters of it. Your fears have no basis. True, the British have fought back in Dimapur, but those are temporary losses. They have relieved the siege at Jotsoma, but that was not significant. Naturally they now try to push further. But they will be stopped. Our men are dug into very good positions on higher ground between the British advance and us. We will prevail.'

Sato's temper got him up and shouting again. 'They have aircraft! They are bombing those very good positions you are talking about! Our lines do not have enough supplies. They do not have enough food. How long do you think they will hold without us advancing to support them? We should be pushing forward instead of trying to take this one *town*!'

But, ultimately, it was no use. The Colonel, backed by the remote might of 15th Army headquarters, always won. Sato sat back on the rough log seat in the face of, he thought, an unmoving contempt for reality.

The 15th Army had made a smooth and steady march westward through the high mountain trails from Burma into these hills. He remembered the infantrymen: alert, disciplined, proud to be part of an actual invasion, the first move forward from Burma after months of fighting the British leftovers there. Most of the 15th Army was made up of reserve soldiers and reserve soldiers, after all, rarely had the opportunity to be part of an invasion force. That honour always went to frontline troops. But so many frontline men had been lost in China and at sea that the reservists finally got their chance. There had been little resistance to their march, the local villagers running away in fright to leave their homes to be looted by the men. When they reached Kohima town, flush with the momentum of their invasion, and found a ragged band of British and Indian defenders, the Japanese had hit them hard, certain of brushing them off and carrying the momentum westward to the plains. Who would have known that it would come to this?

The defenders had retreated, yes, but slowly, ultimately driven now to a small perimeter on top of *Inu* Hill and a few pockets here and there. But even then we would have prevailed, thought Sato: we had more men, we had more and bigger guns, we had more ammunition. Then, out of the western sky, almost, had appeared a *British* Regiment, making its way through our *advancing* lines and had joined the defenders, shoring up the defences. How had that happened? Where did we go wrong? And now the British were massing on the other side of the hills and would move east, were already moving.

Supplies were another problem. British and American bombers were hitting supply convoys behind their lines again and again. Transporting anything, from food to medical supplies to guns and ammunition, was anyhow a problem through these mountains from Burma. The bombings meant only a few convoys made it through intact.

In a bid to please this insufferable man, Sato had left his field post and come down to the Colonel's on another, not that it had done much good. That was another thing: a special station, bunker almost, for a special man, indeed. Valuable troops who should be fighting were posted around him. For what? Sato had asked. To report to me, the Colonel had said. But why take artillery and machine guns when they were needed for fighting?

'Colonel Mori, I must ask you to release some of the men under your command here for deployment along the siege lines. I must also ask you to release the artillery pieces you have deployed around here.'

'General Sato, that is not possible. They have been deployed around this position to secure our communications through radio with headquarters. We cannot risk losing contact with them.'

There was an equally powerful radio at Sato's command post, he could have pointed out. But 15th Army headquarters wanted nothing to do with him.

The only thing you want to secure, Sato thought, looking at the Colonel with increasing fury, is your own skin.

But here, too, there was nothing to be done.

*

The boy was happy. The ponies were one reason for it.

There were three ponies with gunny sacks on them, goatskin bags of water and some boxes. These he would see later. The ponies, he had been told, were part of some transport group in the hills which had gone missing and were probably reported so with the British. The British loved keeping records. What actually happened and what finally went into those reports were vastly different.

They had met the other group on a forest trail leading off from Mokokchung Road, six men and the ponies. His bamboo and box were tied on to one of the ponies. He was happy he didn't have to carry the weight for a while.

The new additions to the group carried their machetes or *nok*s, scabbarded in bamboo, on their backs. These were nearly four feet in length with broad, curving blades narrowing gradually to the long hilt so the *nok* could be comfortably used in a two-handed grip. The hilt was decorated with parallel stripes and triangles. The Konyak had brought his different-looking, axe-like *nok* with him, the tip of the blade flaring out at an angle and becoming a broad head.

They had climbed down to a stony, half-dry creek and followed it south for a while. The hills here were steep but would surely get steeper further south, where the real mountains and the mists began. Thick groves of teak, balsam, kapok and other good timber trees came down almost to the banks of the creek, but there were trails everywhere, beaten down over the years by tribes and plainsmen. They were walking in a loose group, evenly spaced from one another with the ponies at the centre. Two of the men were much further ahead and higher along the hills on either side, scouting the path. One followed, again much behind the group. These three were invisible to the main body of the walkers. They had to watch all sides. The scouts and the follower would rotate with the rest of the group through the march.

This was familiar country for Gojen. He had been up and down much of the Ao lands. This part of the walk would be easy, but he was still happy the rifle was not slowing him down.

He was also happy because Imnuk had come with the second group. Things would surely go all right now.

Imnukluba, too, was the son of an Ao chief. Gojen had met him the first time he went to stay at the *morung*. They had gone on ponies then too, Uti and he, with Uti's grandfather, and a tall young Ao was standing to the side of a trail, straight and motionless, looking at them. Gojen had realised afterward that the man had seen them coming from far away and had been standing motionless since then. The sunlight had filtered down through the leaves that morning and if the grandfather had not called out, the two boys would have never seen him.

Imnuk, along with the elders, had taught them how to hunt and track and use some of the weapons. He had explained to them how each different animal thought and how the hunter must outwit the animal at every turn. He used to say, 'When you hunt, you are placing your hunger against the animal's desire to live. If your hunger is greater, you will get him. But, not always.'

But, not always. That came every time at the end of each lesson, in case the two greenhorns ever thought the teachings would always apply in the world.

Imnuk had a clear, unlined face, unlike many Aos in their early thirties who had wrinkles. He had many stories to tell too, which he would narrate in a humorous, mocking tone, laughing always at the right parts with his listeners.

He was a champion athlete, swift and strong, running, leaping shrubs and fallen trees and swerving through the forest with the boys. Gojen had always wanted to be like him. So had Uti. Eventually, Uti became the good athlete, but Gojen with the rifle was better than Imnuk himself.

The boy's face had lit up when he saw the hunter standing with the ponies.

They were walking side by side now along the creek. Imnuk had accepted with a shrug and a knowing smile when the boy explained how he had joined them. Their chief would cause trouble for them when they returned, but you could not have stopped the boy. Imnuk expected nothing less from his student. They had not talked about Uti.

But he agreed with Meren. 'That was not safe, sitting by the road reading maps. When you are acting a part, you must become the part. And you must always be alert. Always. Particularly where we are going. I am not going to lose both my best students.'

The thought, spoken aloud, was sobering.

'Do you know what is happening there?'

'The British are winning in Dimapur. Some of them are trying to reach Kohima now. Maybe they will reach there by the time we do. That will make things more difficult. But we will be warned and we will avoid anywhere there is fighting along the way. We will have to walk a long way east to avoid the hills between Dimapur and Kohima.'

Somewhere far above them in the skies, a sortie roared eastward.

'Do you think we will find him?'

'We will try. I can't say anything more definite than that.' That was Imnuk: honest, realistic, practical. He would never raise false hopes.

They crossed the creek at a ford of irregular stones worn smooth by the water and walked along the slope of the other hill. A monkey called in the distance. Birds chirped drowsily in the afternoon. It was turning into a good day to walk. The boy yawned, pulling his satchel tighter on his back.

Meren called a halt at a clearing on a slope from where they could see into the distance. The gentler slopes of the hills here allowed them to see far. Nothing was moving among the trees below. The scouts returned and signalled that it was safe.

The boxes were opened. Inside were rifles.

'Lee-Enfields ...' said the boy.

'Like yours, but these are new,' said Imnuk, helping to break open the boxes and tie the rifles with ropes inside gunny sacks. Easier to carry and get ready for use.

'And these are Stens, aren't they?'

They were: six new British-made sub-machine guns, with smooth bare barrels covered by perforated sleeves and thin, long magazines that stuck out vertically from the chamber, unlike other guns. They had a stripped-down look to them. There were also some grenades and medical supplies.

'Where did you get them?' the boy asked.

'We borrowed some from the Ingraz,' Imnuk said and winked.

'The aircraft drop them to their soldiers in the hills. Some are found by the soldiers. Others by the Japani. We thought it would be better if we had them,' explained Meren, loading the rifles on the ponies. 'When our people volunteered with the Ingraz, they were given muskets and told to go and find Japani positions. Have you seen those muskets? They load from the muzzle. You have to reload each time you fire. They are useless and dangerous. But the Ingraz say, take these muskets and fight the Japani. Track them down in the forests, where they are waiting with machine guns and mortars and fight them with muskets. Now we have these and we will be punished if the Ingraz find out.' He shook his head.

'How many boxes are there?'

'In the hills? The planes fly all over every day. There are many such hidden boxes everywhere, from our hills down to the Sangtams'. The Ingraz don't care how many they lose so long as their soldiers get what they want. Many boxes.'

Enough boxes with automatic and bolt-action rifles and grenades to fight an entire war.

Gojen got his bamboo burden down from the pony. He pulled out his knife from his pocket, reversed the grip and smashed the mud cover in with the hilt. He shook the rifle out. A thick smell of Spencer's Gun Cleaner followed.

Imnuk laughed, coming over to where the boy sat unwrapping the paper from the rifle. 'What did you do, pour the entire bottle into it?'

'I could not bring the bottle. I don't know when I will clean it again. I just had to make sure it stays clean.'

'It will stay clean. The only problem you might have is if it slips from your hands, with all that oil on it,' Imnuk laughed again and slapped his back.

The boy wrapped his rifle in a sack and tied it with jute thread, hoisting it back on the pony. He took the box of tea leaves, pried the nails from the cover using the blunt end of the knife blade. One after the other, he took out the paper-wrapped cartridges and dropped them in his satchel.

The men finished their unloading, covering the guns on the horses' backs with more gunny sacks. The bamboo and the broken boxes were pushed deep inside a clump of shrubs. Meren took the box of tea and hammered the lid back down.

'You won't throw it away?' the boy asked.

'We might have tea later,' said Meren, placing the box inside his satchel. Gojen found this amusing. He thought only Englishmen talked of having tea while going off to war.

They swung up the incline and headed south once again.

The hills in the distance were growing taller. It was getting colder.

Evening came soon after.

10

'You are not thinking about Uti, are you?' Meren asked.

They were lying on their backs, heads on their satchels, lying on blankets with more blankets covering them, in another small clearing. The nights were getting cooler the further they walked.

A small fire of branches, twigs and dry grass had died out. The ponies were standing under a tree nearby, sleeping. There were fewer mosquitoes the higher they went, but they still rubbed semi-dry citronella leaves on themselves to keep the insects away.

Gojen had been looking at the stars which shone bright in the clear night sky, thinking of similar nights when his friend and he had watched the stars and talked of the many new things they had seen in the village and forests, laughing at the mannerisms of some odd villager or the pranks they had pulled.

So, Elephant, you ran away from home and here you are under the stars again. Very clever of you, you must be thinking, whispered Uti. *Do you even know what you are going to do?*

No, I don't, Uti, the boy thought. Since you always knew more than I did, why don't you tell me now, instead of pulling my leg?

They had made good progress before night had set in. They lit a fire, threw in some rice and dried pork strips and had a filling dinner. The pork strips were cured and lasted a long time and were therefore preferred by travellers. They also tasted good, particularly when eaten with rock salt. It was the first full meal of the day, since they had only eaten some pork strips in the afternoon.

Two of the men were once again on watch at either end of the hill.

'A little bit.' There wasn't much to say. What was the point?

'I want you to stop feeling sad, at least till we finish the work. Where we are going you will have to think clearly all the time. You might even have to act quickly. I don't want you to make any mistakes and hurt yourself.'

'Meren,' said the boy, turning his head to look at the Naga, 'do you think the war will ever end?'

Meren began to smile until he remembered the war had been around since the boy was ten. 'It will end here soon. The Ingraz will not allow the Japani to push into your valley. The Japani are not as strong as they were when they came to Burma, I am told. I don't know when fighting in other places will end.'

'What was it like, when you were in France?'

'That was … different.'

In the thick of the First World War, four thousand Nagas had volunteered in the British Army, and the Naga Labour Corps was formed and sent to France. Meren had been one of them, a young man.

'At first we worked as labour in the British lines. Some of us also took rifles and fought if we were required. But mostly we were transporting food and guns. We were on a plain. The whole area was burnt: there were no trees or grass anywhere. We used to take supplies on horsecarts through the mud to the trenches. Everywhere there were long, deep trenches and dirty, thin men. Some of the men were not wounded but they just could not fight. They were frightened or something. The doctors said they were of no use, so they were sent home.'

'What had happened to them?'

'Some said the sound of the big guns, the fighting, the screams, drove them out of their minds. I saw some of these men. I think it was a different reason. All these men, Ingraz, French, they were just young boys. They lived in nice, comfortable houses and ate good food. When they heard about the war they joined the Army, thinking war is some glorious adventure. But then they found that fighting is just a dirty, bloody, hard thing. I think they were just not ready to see how ugly these things are.'

'But you hadn't fought before and you were not affected, were you?'

'That was because I had no expectations at all. I just volunteered and went. I did not know about their politics and had nothing to do with the causes. When the enemy fired, I put my head down and tried not to get killed. I just did my work.'

'You didn't join the Club afterwards.'

Meren raised his head. 'Who told you about the Club? Your grandfather?'

The boy nodded.

The First World War had been the Nagas' first big entry on to the world's stage. The Labour Corps members had seen Europe at first-hand and come back to tell their people about the world. A new consciousness was growing in the hills. The corpsmen and educated young Nagas who returned from the war formed the Naga Club, a political society. They had gone from village to village, tribe to tribe, talking with the headmen and the elders, discussing the conditions in which the tribesmen lived. They would occasionally meet with the British Deputy Commissioner for the Naga Hills, at his office in Kohima, and present their suggestions and requests. They were beginning to get things done in the hills, the boy had heard.

'No, I didn't join the Club. I didn't want anything to do with talking with the Ingraz, asking for their help. But I support the Club and what they are doing. If it helps our people, it is good.'

'Meren, what will happen to the hills when the war is over?'

'Why do you ask?'

'Everyone says India might even become free after the war. The British will leave us and go away.'

Meren snorted. 'They have been talking about that for a long time, much before you were born. But maybe things will be different this time. The Ingraz are fighting all around the world. London has been bombed so many times, hasn't it? Maybe by the time the fighting ends, they will be too tired or damaged to want to stay on. Who knows?'

'But they are fighting to stop the Japanese from occupying the hills, aren't they? The hills are under the British, aren't they?'

'Boy, the Ingraz came here because they wanted to create protection for India. A buffer area, they call it. They came to your lands for the wood and coal and oil. The hills are under them, yes, but the hills don't belong to them, because they do not really love the hills. It is not their home. You have to belong to the land before the land can belong to you.' He looked again at the boy. 'You must understand this too.'

'Then what will happen, when the British leave?'

'We will have our hills as we had them in the past. The Club says we, all the tribes, must unite into one people. I think it might be to our advantage.'

The boy thought it would be something to see, all the tribes uniting. But there would be difficulties.

'What does Shilukaba say?'

'He is of an older generation. He thinks only of the Ao. That is good, even in this case. He thinks working together with the other tribes would be good for us. But there are many things to sort out first.'

'And what happens if some other army comes in after the British leave?'

'Who will come in, once the Japani are defeated?'

Gojen connected the dots here rather rapidly.

'Meren?'

'Hmm?'

'All those boxes you said were dropped by the British and never found. Who is keeping an eye on them? There is someone storing and distributing them, isn't there? I mean, you said there were so many of the boxes all over the hills. One tribe can't know where they all are. The Club is collecting them, isn't it?'

'Yes. The Club is very busy now. But these boxes we got ourselves.'

Someone poked the boy's ribs. He turned around. Imnuk had been lying down, eyes closed, awake, listening to the conversation.

'If you want to show us how clever you are at guessing things, why don't you do it in the morning, Rajkhowa? Unless you want to go on guard duty and yawn all tomorrow morning like you did today.'

Naturally the boy didn't want that.

He turned around and lay on his back again, looking at the stars. A buckle on the bag pressed against his head. He reached behind and adjusted it. A leaf of grass, cold in the night, pressed against his ear and tickled him. He brushed it away but it returned. He pushed the stem under his blanket.

He would have to take it one thing at a time. He would have to do well whatever he was doing at the moment, and take the next task and do that, and so on. He had taken a leap into the unknown and now he would just have to go on and see what was to be seen.

He could not afford to get tired if he was to keep up with the men. He had to sleep.

The next morning began early: the ponies were packed and they were moving much before dawn, this time once again along the shoulder of the hills, sometimes along creek banks. They would not allow him to go ahead with the other scouts. He was nearing the limit of his known world.

The early afternoon also brought good news.

Imnuk signalled the others to stop when they had crossed another creek and were heading into a tree clump. The boy strained his ears and thought he heard a faint rustling among the trees. He looked at the others, his brow furrowed in a question, but did not ask anything.

Imnuk whispered something to Meren, went to one of the ponies and unwrapped a bundle. He took out a crossbow and a bunch of iron-tipped arrows. The beam of the bow, on which the arrows were fitted to the bowstring, pulled back against a hook and launched, was already fixed to the arch of the bow. Imnuk liked to carry the crossbow ready for use, the boy remembered.

The hunter stepped lightly towards the trees, stopped for a moment and listened. He went in. The boy wanted to follow but didn't; he had not been told to and Imnuk did not like people getting in his way while hunting.

'What is it?' asked the Konyak in a low whisper. Amazingly, he had not said a word over the whole march the previous day or this morning.

'Wild pig, he says,' replied Meren.

'Up here? I didn't know they were up so high in the hills too,' the Konyak remarked.

'There are not as many of them here as in the valleys. But it can't be a boar; a boar would make more noise or none at all and you need a lot of men to chase it down, if it does not rush at you first. Hogs are easier.'

The rustling broke out louder and clearer, but they heard only the animal, not the man hunting it. Gojen pictured it in his mind: Imnuk tracing the animal's movement, approaching slowly and soundlessly, throwing a stone to misguide it and make it run nearer, his crossbow ready, firing ...

There was a single high squeak.

Imnuk came out of the trees a while later, smiling, the hog slung over his shoulder. It was large for a wild pig, but small for a domestic one. But it was fresh food. He slung it over a pony, roped it down and covered it with a blanket to keep away the flies.

A little later they stopped for lunch. They lit a fire and roasted the hog, sprinkling just a little rock salt on the meat because too much rock salt spoilt the taste.

The group was happy. It was always nice to get fresh meat while travelling, and the meat really tasted good. A good hunt also brought out the storyteller in everyone, night or day. And it was a good day to eat and tell stories.

112

Even the Konyak finally seemed to want to talk.

'I didn't even hear the animal,' he admitted to Imnuk as they sat around the fire. The scouts had returned to their posts with the food.

'But that is Imnuk. When I travel with him, I don't have to worry about anything. He sees and hears and smells for everyone,' said one of the men, laughing.

'Everyone from the Tsitir clan of our tribe is like that, Konyak. They are good hunters, next only to my clan, the Azukamr,' said Meren.

'Yes, and the most special thing about them is they are difficult to kill,' someone said, as the Aos laughed again.

'That is not true,' said Imnuk, his face serious. 'The truth is, men of my clan can't be killed in a fight.'

The group laughed again.

'Why is that?' asked the Konyak, chewing the meat. He did not know many of the stories of the Ao tribe, naturally. The boy did. This was one of the most amazing stories he had ever heard at the *morung*.

Imnuk ladled a big helping of rice from the pot, chewed on the pork and looked thoughtful.

'This is a very old story. It happened sometime during the early days of the Ao tribe, my mother said. One morning, two men went fishing in a river in the northern hills.'

'And they caught many minnows,' interrupted one of his listeners. It always happened during storytelling: everyone who knew the story would interrupt to make his own contribution.

'And they caught many small minnows, yes,' agreed Imnuk. 'They were good fishermen. They took some of the fish and put them inside a bamboo. Then they corked one end of the bamboo with leaves, like some people do even today when they don't have anything to cook meat in. They placed the bamboo over a fire and waited a while.

'Then they uncorked the bamboo. But when they tipped it to one side, they found that the fish inside weren't cooked at all ...'

'Far from being cooked, the fish were still alive,' another listener told the Konyak, eager to tell the strange part himself.

'The two men, naturally, were puzzled,' Imnuk said patiently, chewing the rice. 'But they could not explain it. So they got some more leaves, corked the bamboo and placed it over the fire again ...'

'And this time ...' someone began, but Imnuk was quick.

'And this time, when they uncorked the bamboo, they found the fish had been cooked,' the hunter said. 'So they started thinking about the whole thing. They put the fish inside once more, corked the bamboo with the earlier leaves and cooked it a third time. And this time, when they opened it, they found the fish were alive once more!'

The Konyak was listening intently.

'From this the two men realised that the leaves could bring the dead to life. They took the secret of the leaves to their clan, the Tsitir. Soon, with the help of the leaves, the clan became powerful. But some other clans became jealous of the rise of the Tsitirs. So they ambushed them and killed all the men. Everyone, except a little baby boy.

'His mother, in order to save him from the other clans, shaved his hair, pretended that he was a little girl, took him away and hid him in the forest, where he grew up as a hunter. Then she told him the story of his clan and asked him to take back his rights in the tribe. None of the men in the other clans dared to pick a fight with him because of his strength and courage. So he went on and founded the clan once again. But in all this, the secret of the leaves which gave life was lost.

'However, they say that in place of these magic leaves, the men of my clan got a new power—they couldn't be killed in a fight,' Imnuk said, finishing his meal and getting up.

'They only say that, you know. It is only a story,' said someone.

'It could be true, though,' said another, laughing. 'You know why? Because the Tsitir never fight, anyway. They are too busy hunting and making honey from beehives.'

Imnuk just shook his head dismissively at the joke.

'But Imnuk, please remember that my clan did not kill those men, all right?' teased one of the men.

'Neither did mine. These are old stories, aren't they, Imnuk? Just in case you get angry with me later,' said another, laughing with the rest at the hunter, who had his back turned to them, getting the ponies ready for the next march.

'It is a good story,' said the Konyak to one of the men near him.

'There are many stories in our tribe you haven't heard of,' the man replied.

'Yes,' said another, 'Meren's clan's story, for instance.'

'Meren is an Azukamr. Have you heard the name, Konyak?' asked the first one.

'Yes. They are important in your tribe, aren't they?'

'They are very important,' said the man. Meren was some distance away, pulling at the reins of one of the ponies. 'The story says that the great hero Shiluti once had a dog, a fast and strong hunting dog. One day, the dog got lost. Shiluti looked everywhere for it and called for it, but could not find it. He was sad because it had been such a valuable and loyal dog.

'The next morning, when Shiluti was out walking in the forest, he heard a voice calling out to him. He went looking for the source of the voice. He came across a man with half his body trapped inside a hollow log. The hero got down to help the man, but the man said, "I am your dog. I am now turning into a man, but it is only half complete. Please go away and return tomorrow."

'The great hero returned to the spot the following day and found the man was complete and free from the log. He took the man to his house and adopted him as his son. He became the first of the Azukamr clan, and they have always been lieutenants to Shiluti's descendants since. You can identify them by a scar they have somewhere on their body. But don't ask Meren about it.'

'Is that why he was chosen to lead this group?' the Konyak asked.

'That could be one reason,' the Ao said. 'Anyway, he is the best man to lead us. He knows all the places and everything about the Ingraz. He is very clever.'

'Was he close to the boy who died?' the Konyak asked.

But no one wanted to talk about the dead at the moment. There were too many, and it was too recent.

A few birds chirped in the trees. A group of monkeys was seen at a distance, climbing among the branches. Though one had not been sighted, this was hoolock gibbon country. These animals spent most of their lives without coming down from the trees. The Aos had long protected the gibbon because its numbers were falling.

The forest from here started becoming a thick tangle of ferny undergrowth and mossy rock. These were big, green ferns with primeval edges like saws. Primeval was the right word, Gojen thought, remembering from science lessons that ferns were a very old species, virtually unchanged by evolution. The leaves had always impressed him since his early childhood, with their look of age and menace; he sometimes even had dreams of dense ferns swaying in the night, swaying and parting in the wind ...

They were now walking in a rough south-eastern direction, as Meren had said earlier, to avoid the fighting around Dimapur. They were still some distance from Angami land, their route now taking them towards the taller mountains of the east, for the Naga hills climb to great heights eastward, with an uneven belt of mountains bisecting the land in a north-south direction. That belt lay further to the east; they would not have to travel through it.

Sometime towards the late evening, one of the scouts emerged from the forest ahead of them and conferred with Meren. The leader held up his hand and signalled them to leave the path and head deeper into the forest.

They came across a clearing and saw the village perched at the edge of a steep ravine. It was a good place to build a village, the boy thought. It commanded a large view of the green hills, while the forest had been cleared back some distance to cultivate a few crops.

They stopped and spread in a wide line. The scout shook his head in answer to a question. There was no one in the village, he said. Nor in the forest around.

It was a small village. Perhaps twenty families had lived here. They were long gone, run away to the plains with what they could carry: food, livestock, *mithan*—Kenneally's 'outsize cows'—pigs, chickens, clothes.

A drum of cowhide—an *asem*, the boy remembered—stood slanted, almost toppling, next to a large hut, probably the headman's. The houses were built Ao-fashion: on wooden stilts.

The village was too small to have a boys' house of its

own. Perhaps the boys went to a *morung* in a bigger village somewhere when they were old enough. Some of the bigger huts were supported with wooden pillars with tigers drawn on them. These were longitudinal views of the tiger sculpted from the top. Uti and Gojen had often joked that they looked more like lizards than ferocious tigers, but that was the way they were always sculpted. Over what Gojen thought was the headman's house was a sculpture of two snakes circling each other in concentric circles, for good luck or some such. It had not worked, obviously.

It had rained here a few days earlier: the bare soil around the huts turned to mud, the water trickling down rocks at the edge of the ravine and leaving marks on the stone. They were entering country where the rains had already begun.

They checked each house. The doors were ajar and, anyway, few such huts had ways of locking them. If you did not trust your neighbour, why live next to him? But there was no one, the few pieces of furniture and cooking pots rolling on the floor where the villagers had abandoned them in their haste to leave.

'It has been empty for a fortnight or so. Does anyone know where the people are?' Meren asked. They must be in a camp in the plains somewhere, but none of the group had heard about people from this village. It was at the edge of Ao lands.

The boy glanced quietly at the Konyak, who stood in the middle of the line of huts, looking around him. What was he thinking about? Perhaps of another village, just like this, far away to the east in the northern mountains of Burma. Was he remembering his family? Who knew what he was feeling now.

Gojen went and stood at the edge of the ravine, looking out towards the distant sky. The only good thing he could feel at the moment was the wind.

Meren spoke with the scout again. They picked up the pace, cutting through the village down to the ravine, where they splashed—softly—across the cold water.

The next hill on the way would have to be climbed over, said Meren. It was too wide to walk around and they had to move quickly now. The men pulled the ponies by their reins up through the trees, which were giving way to oak, some varieties of cherry the boy thought he had seen in the eastern mountains before but wasn't sure, and small clumps of pine. At places the rocks had been worn by forest trails: these were the easy parts. At other places, they had to pull themselves up, balancing with their hands on creepers and wild vines. These were likely places for beehives, the boy recalled, and kept looking around for the little stinging creatures.

The climb downhill, which they made eventually, was steeper and even more difficult for the pony handlers; they had to keep the animals from rushing downhill and colliding with trees and bushes. A narrow, uneven and muddy slope led to the base of the hill from halfway above. They walked down this, catching their breath. It hadn't been as tiring as it looked.

They were now on the western edge of flatter land. In the distance the Jalla river, tributary of the Doyang, rushed north. To the west were the hills of the Lotha and Rengma Nagas. East of the river ran a long unbroken ridge, from where the hills of the Semas began. Straight to the south was Angami land. Conifers were already being seen in large numbers. The hills here rose steeply in long humps, and the trails became more rocky and fern-filled.

It would be another evening on the road soon. Meren told them to walk faster to cover more ground before the night. A scout was walking towards them, with another man identically dressed with a straw hat on his head. One of the runners.

Meren and Imnuk went ahead to talk with them. The others halted, one or two bringing out betel nuts and chewing. Shilukaba had banned opium among his people for a long time, and it was one habit he wanted his people to be rid of completely. Betel nuts, in contrast, were tolerated. The boy wouldn't look at them: they would come back and burn his throat even days afterwards when he was running. He didn't want to have anything to do with any substance that made him feel unpleasant inside.

Imnuk returned while Meren continued talking with the British-employed runner, asking him questions and gesturing.

'What has happened?' someone asked.

'The Ingraz have captured Dimapur. They also bombed the Japani on the road to Kohima. Some Japani have been captured, most have died or fallen back. We have to be more careful from now on. Some Ingraz soldiers have reached Kohima. More will reach there through the night. We have to walk faster.'

Meren returned with the runner.

'Unpack the horses. We will carry the bags ourselves. He ...' gesturing at the runner, 'will take the ponies back to the Ingraz lines. We have a lot of climbing ahead.'

Gojen untied and placed the gunny sack on the ground, squatting next to it. He unwrapped it and worked the bolt once or twice, checking if it was working smoothly. It was always the first thing he checked. Then he detached the magazine, placed it on the satchel—he would *not* get it muddy—took out ten rounds from the bag, unwrapped them, gave each a final polish on his shirt, and inserted them in the magazine. Then he relocked the magazine. He just wanted to be ready. The others were checking their guns and loading as well, Imnuk with one of the Stens fitting a twenty-round magazine to the chamber.

'What is that?' Imnuk asked the boy, pointing at his satchel. He walked over, carrying the Sten, and picked out a roll of cotton from the bag.

'You use this at the range to protect your ears?'

The boy nodded. The hunter tightened the cotton into a ball and threw it away.

'Where we are going, you will have to be alert and listen to everything. Muffling the noise might end up hurting you. We are not going to the range,' said Imnuk, trying to keep the edge off his voice.

The runner took the ponies and started back down his trail. The group moved south-east once again.

The tide was turning. They were walking towards it.

*

Sato could only feel helplessness. The British had made their push forward and were at the point of lifting the Kohima siege. His invasion force's (it was *still* his force, if only on paper) momentum had run out.

'Mori,' he was saying, 'you will tell headquarters that our situation is taking a turn for the worse. We need to take the initiative.'

'And we will, General Sato, we will. As soon as I get a clear idea of the size of the British force, I will have a plan to counter-attack and end their advance ...'

'By the time you get your precious information together, they will have pushed us back into Burma, Mori.'

'General,' said the Colonel, getting up from a cot inside Sato's command bunker and pacing the room, 'your problem is you constantly over-estimate the British. In a day or so, I will have a counter-attack planned and ready. Naturally you will cooperate, as I have assured headquarters.'

And, once again, Sato had been cunningly side-stepped.

121

11

It was dark, but he could see the dazzling greenness of the ferns. This was strange, he thought distantly. The ferns, big, bright green, sharp blades of green on their edges, all around him, swaying in the wind. The wind rose. The ferns were shifting. They were parted and bending towards him and from behind them arose a blackness ...

He opened his eyes and shut them again. He shook his head free from the nightmare. He was lying on his blanket on the slope, in the muddy grass. It was nearing dawn: the sky was bright in patches across the hills.

He woke up with the familiar scratchy feeling on his cheeks from the fuzz growing there. It still took some getting used to. Uti had much less fuzz, but they had both debated what to do with proper beards when they grew, for neither wanted to keep them. Some tribes plucked them out strand by strand, some others, supposedly, even burnt them to solve the problem. Whatever the case, they had different plans ...

He looked around. The men were not there. There was a mess of footprints going into the forest from the spot where they had slept.

What had happened? Had he overslept after the hard climb the night before? Where were they?

He sat up, folded the blankets and stuffed them inside the satchel. He crouched and looked around. There was not a sound in the forest or the sky.

Voices.

He crept forward, still crouching, to the edge of the hillside, next to a fallen log, pushed slowly at the bushes on the edge of the slope and looked out.

Four men were walking up. They had guns. They, too, were dressed in shorts. The guns were different, he saw at once. The clothes too: green with markings on them. One of the men looked up towards where he crouched.

Japanese soldiers.

Here was the enemy, in the flesh, four with guns, growing larger by the minute. His mouth went dry.

He saw everything with a clearness he had never felt, not even while hunting. The men in green, climbing upwards, guns slung on their backs, pouches at their belts containing, no doubt, bullets and whatnot, the hills behind them, the dawn creeping slowly across the skies. A sparrow chirruped somewhere. It was a sparrow, he was sure of it.

They are coming towards *me*! They will keep climbing and *see me*! Where are the men?

They were closer now. He looked around. He could try running. He could crouch lower and hope they would turn away. They hadn't seen him yet. He still had a chance. *Where are the men?*

His hand searched downwards in the grass, his eyes still on the Japanese. His hands found his rifle. Ten bullets in the magazine. He had his gun.

He pulled it towards himself, slowly, his heart sitting somewhere just behind his teeth by now. He gripped the rifle and angled it forward, the muzzle just short of the edge of the bushes. *Never show the rifle. Never push it out.* If it worked for deer, it could work for …

He sighted down the barrel, locked both his hands in the proper position on top of the log, looking down at the soldiers. He hadn't zeroed the sight yet, but at this height and distance …

He pushed the bolt forward as he had done countless times before. He heard the chamber close on the round. He placed his index finger on the trigger, pulled it back, felt the tension on the tiny piece of metal. He pulled.

For the first time in his life, he shot at a *man*.

For the first time in his life, he missed.

He almost *saw* the bullet fly over the head of the man he had aimed at, hitting a shrub just behind him and smashing into it with the sound of wet leaves.

The soldiers stopped and crouched immediately, looked upwards, shouted and began running. Towards him. Two of them fired wildly, the bullets going high over the bushes.

Gojen fell back, his mind near panic. More shots came. He began pushing backwards, kicking his heels into the mud. Then a large hand caught him by the neck, stopping him. He gave a shout.

'Shh!' It was Meren, crouched beside him, finger on his lips. He pointed towards the bushes and moved forward. The boy followed him. There were more shots but not close. The soldiers hadn't seen his exact position.

He parted the bushes once again, even more cautiously than before. A valley sparrow chirruped. This time he was doubly sure it was a sparrow. Another sparrow chirruped. Sparrows everywhere.

As far as he knew, there were no valley sparrows in the southern hills of the Ao.

The soldiers were scrambling up. The bushes behind

124

them were pushed outwards. Six men were standing up, running silently out of the bushes, *noks* raised.

The boy turned around and leaned back against the log, breathing heavily, little jolts of a sharp, warm feeling deep inside his stomach.

The shivering started in a few moments.

He was sitting on the log clasping his arms close to his chest, feeling miserable, when five of the group showed up. With them was a young Naga of average height, also in scout uniform and straw hat. He had fairer skin than the Aos, and a clear, unlined face. He walked with his head high and proud, clearly used to leading and deciding. He was from a different tribe, Gojen saw immediately.

Meren and Imnuk were talking with him in quick sentences and the three men were smiling about something, perhaps over a remark Imnuk had made. They walked up to where the boy was sitting. The newcomer looked the boy up and down and noticed the rifle at his side.

'Rajkhowa,' said the young man. His voice was smooth but he rolled his r's. He was clearly less used to Assamese names than the Aos. He crouched next to Gojen. 'Welcome to the hills of the Angami,' he said in English. It was spoken fairly well, hinting at a school education under British missionaries.

The boy took the offered hand and shook it. The man had clearly been meeting a lot of British.

Then he understood. The men who had burst out of the trees behind the Japanese soldiers were Angami tribesmen. This was their leader. The travellers had reached the Angami hills, possibly during the night. The 'hosts' had welcomed them. It was an elaborate courtesy extended by each tribe to any newcomer to their hills.

Even more, the boy inferred, the Angamis must have

known the reason behind their coming. Had they come out to meet them? The times must really be changing in the hills, he thought, when two important tribes were cooperating on a mission like this.

The Angami guessed the questions in the boy's mind. 'We had been following the Japani since they escaped from a position near Dimapur yesterday evening. They were probably lost and could not contact the rest of their unit. These Japani,' he said, smiling and turning to Imnuk, 'they don't know anything about finding directions in the hills. Particularly the men. I doubt the officers are any better. As long as it is a big road or trail marked on their maps, they are fine. Otherwise, they just walk around in circles. They can't even navigate by the sun.' The Ao hunter laughed at this.

'Anyhow, we followed them through the night, thinking they might meet more of their men. Better than us searching for them, you know. Then you fired and we had to stop them,' he ended simply.

'I missed,' Gojen said, his voice small, confused. He looked at Imnuk who looked back but didn't reply.

'Actually, it was good you fired when you did, and not later,' the young Angami said. 'If you had, you might have hit me,' he added, smiling at the thought.

'I missed,' the boy said again.

But Meren was talking now. 'He is the son of the chief of Keuhira village,' he said, pointing at the new man and using the old name for Kohima.

'My father sent me with these men to wait for you on the Kohima trail, just south of here,' the man explained.

Son of the chief. It seemed they were all sons of chiefs in the group, indicating the seriousness of this mission. In all the accounts of the tribes, the boy thought, this was the first time he had heard of them working together like this. Then he remembered, that under the old Ahom military nobility system, 'Rajkhowa' was a rank equivalent to 'general', so that was all right.

Suddenly, the boy also pieced together what must have happened. The scouts his group had posted must have seen the Japanese soldiers and behind them, they would have seen the silent band tracking them. The scouts had warned his group, who had separated into the forests to watch what would follow.

Meren and the newcomer went off to talk to the other Angamis. Imnuk sat down by the boy's side.

'But you could have told me,' Gojen said to his teacher.

'What about?'

'You could have told me that the soldiers were coming this way. I woke up and found you were gone.'

'And when you saw the soldiers, you became afraid.'

'I became afraid.'

Imnuk put his hand around the boy's shoulders. 'Meren wanted to wake you up too, but I said, let him see the soldiers on his own. We wanted to see what you would do.'

The boy looked at him, almost as angry as he could get, which was not much.

'It was a test?'

'A very small one. We didn't want you to panic later. Anyhow, no one was in danger. The Angamis had been ready for the soldiers all through last night.'

A test. He had done badly, hadn't he?

'I panicked.'

'No. Try to remember. You saw the soldiers. You didn't see us. You didn't see the Angamis either. And don't tell this to our new friend, but they need to practise tracking. They were not as silent as they should have been. Anyway, I'll tell you what you did. You thought you had been left alone, for whatever reason, and the soldiers were climbing towards you. You had the rifle. You fired. I would have done the same. It is all right. You did well in the position you found yourself.' He patted his student's back.

'But I missed.'

Imnuk considered this for a while, theatrically stretching his legs, first one then the other, locking his fingers and cracking the knuckles, backward, a sign that he was getting his thoughts in a row. 'I would have been surprised if you hadn't. You were firing at a man, remember? It is very different than practising at your range or firing at a bird or a wild pig. You might not remember thinking about it, but at the back of the mind you always think: I am shooting at a *man*. He is just like me. I am shooting at a person. In this case, though,' he added with a laugh to humour the boy, 'a slightly dirtier person than yourself.'

'I don't remember thinking anything.'

'But you did. From the moment you aimed to the moment you pulled the trigger, it was going on inside your mind. You were trying to save your own life, but it is still a difficult thing to do, firing at a man, even when he is armed.'

'Imnuk,' said the boy, smiling at the Ao, 'you talk as if you have been hunting men instead of wild boar all your life.'

'Maybe I have. What do you know?' Imnuk said seriously. That shut the boy up.

'Do you think that is what happened?' Gojen asked in a bit.

'I am sure of it. Maybe it does something to the fingers or the hand. I don't know. Maybe it makes you hasty. You miss.'

'Then it could happen again.'

'Listen. You are not here to fight. We, Meren and I,

have two important things to remember, and I will tell the Angami this too. First is to find the Japani officer ...'

'Mori.'

'The Japani officer Mori. The second is to make sure you don't get hurt. If it looks like you might, we will go back. I told you before: I won't lose both my best students.'

'But what if ...'

'What if nothing. When we reach there, you use your eyes and your head, not that finger. You won't be near any Japani soldiers again.'

'But what if it happens?'

Imnuk sighed. He wasn't good at arguing. 'All right. If, once again, for instance, you wake up one morning alone on a hillside and find four lost Japani soldiers climbing up a hill towards you, the first thing you must do is stay calm. Consider everything. If they have not seen you, there is no need to tell them that you are there. If it is necessary, such as if they are coming towards you like just now, or if they are looking for you, only then must you use the rifle. But you know that just because you are carrying that toy of yours does not mean you *have* to use it.

'When you aim, forget everything else. Just aim like you have always done before, get the position correct, do all the things you know. Then, you go inside yourself. Find a small place there that tells you: aim and fire, don't miss. It does not matter what you are firing at, just *don't miss*. That small place does not have any feeling. That small place does not tell you that this is a human being so let us get up and wave to him and he will wave back and smile and not shoot. If you can find it, stay inside that place and fire. But,' he said, getting up and brushing the muddy grass from his ankles, 'I only tell you because you asked.'

Will you remember that now, stupid Elephant? said Uti, sitting beside him. *You look like all the ghosts in the hills have been chasing you. You are not going to lose your head at an important moment, are you?*

Uti, what happened to you at the village? the boy asked him. *What did you think when the firing started? What did you do when the people started dying? You were alone. You were hiding. You didn't have a gun ...*

You don't need a gun all *the time, Elephant,* Uti whispered back. *I had what I needed. I managed.*

You did what you could. I don't know what I will do if I meet the Japanese again.

I thought so. It looks like I will have to help you again, Elephant. You are so clumsy on your own.

He had a lot of thinking to do.

The Angami had unfolded a British military map, complete with elevation lines, and was explaining matters to the group. The map mainly showed a long snake winding around the page.

'This is Imphal Road,' he said, indicating the snake. It went with a few small curves from west to east and took a sharp ninety-degree turn to the south, running down and exiting the page.

'This,' he said, pointing at a group of circles along the east-west stretch and south of the road, 'is IGH Spur, under the Ingraz. The Japanese had surrounded them, but reinforcements have arrived.'

At the point where the road took the sharp turn south was another circle, just west of the road. 'This is Garrison Hill. The DC's house is here and so are most of the Ingraz. This is where the fighting is heaviest.' The Japanese lines were close to the British, Gojen noted.

Imphal Road, going south, crossed a small islet of sorts, surrounded by a small hill track. At its centre was another group of British defenders. 'That is Jail Hill. They are far from being relieved,' said the Angami. 'From the plan you have told me, our best chance is here.'

That was another hill west of Imphal Road, where Japanese lines were deep. 'We think Japani officers are somewhere on that hill. If we can find our way up there, we have a chance.'

'Once we reach Kohima Ridge, which is the quickest way to this place?' Meren asked.

'All the parts south and west of Imphal Road are not safe. There are Ingraz and Japani soldiers everywhere. If they don't get you, the big guns will. The best way is,' he pointed at the upper right corner of the map, opposite Garrison Hill, 'through here. From this line of hills in the north, if we cut across the village opposite Garrison Hill and climb the Eastern Ridge. This part has no soldiers. Otherwise, west or east, soldiers everywhere.'

The Eastern Ridge was a continuous mountain which paralleled the north-south stretch of Imphal Road. Every other place on the map seemed full of Japanese patrols.

'Why are there no soldiers there?'

'They can't carry artillery up that ridge. It is too steep. But we can climb and go south along it.'

'Through the village first?'

'That's the only safe way if you don't want to be caught and questioned by the Ingraz.' He looked at the guns they carried. 'And you can't explain those.'

'But there is fighting in the town and village too,' objected an Ao.

'Till two days ago. The Ingraz pushed the Japani back. They are still shelling Ingraz positions in the village, but it is the safest way. You will only have to run quickly. Once we reach this point here on the Eastern Ridge, we can cross Imphal Road and move towards their general headquarters.

But we will have to find it first. That will be the difficult part.'

More discussions followed. The boy lost interest, mainly because they were talking about places and people he did not know much of. He went and sat on the log.

Imnuk came up. He had found a rough stone and was using it to sharpen his hunting knife.

'Gojen.'

'Hmm?'

'You stay close to me. We might have to do a lot of running, down one ridge, through the village and up this other one. Big guns will be firing. Stay close and follow what I tell you to do,' he said without looking up from his work.

'All right.'

Gojen, for want of anything else to do, took out his knife from his pocket. It was identical to another made for Uti. Both had been made by the best bladesmith in the Ao hills, a man in Mokokchung.

The piece of iron was said to have been brought from Burma, where the tribes could get good iron. The blade had been beaten, hammered and folded into a uniform thickness up and down. The blade, whose blunt end curved outward from the tip before dipping back, went down to the very end of the hilt, which was made of polished kapok wood. By placing a finger beneath the edge where blade met hilt, he could balance the knife. It was, in effect, a throwing knife resembling a gralloch knife, and combined both purposes. His throwing arm was good, but not as good as Uti's.

It was sharp. It had a good blade. He had good equipment with him, he reflected. He just had to see if he was ready for what was to come.

'You are thinking again, boy. Just make sure you don't forget to see and hear.'

Gojen made a gesture.

'What?' the hunter asked.

'Give me your stone when you are finished.'

Towards the afternoon, as they were crossing the shoulder of a particularly steep and pine-covered hill, it began to rain. Fat drops of rainwater fell thick and fast. They sheltered under a rocky overhang, checking their weapons and food, listening to the spatter of drops on rock and tree and leaf. They had been fortunate it had not rained as often as it usually did.

Late in the afternoon they reached an amphitheatre of towering hills.

'Kohima beyond this,' said the Angami, gesturing.

Far away, they heard the noise of battle.

12

'Ready?' Imnuk asked.

They were crouching at the top of Northern Ridge, looking down on the village. Some of the men, leaving their guns behind, had walked casually down through the village and up into Eastern Ridge without being stopped. Others, carrying guns, would try their luck in small groups through the evening and into the night. Imnuk, as he had promised, was going across with the boy. But Gojen's attention was elsewhere.

Two giants, it seemed, had crashed together with devastating force at Kohima and then wrestled up and down the hills. For as far as he could see (and from the hilltop he could see very far) there was no green: it was a complete uniform black and grey mudscape. The few trees that had not been cut down or blown apart by shells stood forlorn and bare, their blackened branches lifted up to the grey skies like skinny fingers.

'Garrison Hill,' said Imnuk, pointing a cautious finger.

Across a narrow muddy track—so this was the famous Imphal Road, the boy thought—that circled it in a tight arc, a steep incline could be seen. It was dotted with moving and crouching men. Deep gashes could be seen in the earth—these were trenches from where men fired down the hill with machine guns and rifles. The base of the hill was surrounded by another line of trenches, lined with rough slabs of stone. These were Japanese soldiers.

A short distance from the base of their hilltop, they could see the village on their side of Imphal Road. It was a mad jumble of huts and a few small houses, some of them destroyed by the shells. Japanese positions were even now shelling British trenches lining the village.

The air was choking and acrid, full of woodsmoke and gunsmoke, Kohima's famed healthy high-altitude air ruined by over a fortnight of exploding shells. A thousand hammers were driving nails into hard wood all over the ridgeline. A hundred woodpeckers were knocking their hungry beaks on a hundred trees.

'Those are Japani heavy machine guns. They sound like woodpeckers,' explained Imnuk. 'They sound like they fire slowly, but the bullets are heavy.'

But the constant, the completely masterful, the god-like, was artillery. Mortar shells were flying from a dozen positions on every hillside. Where they struck, they exploded with a hollow boom. The brisance of the explosive in the shells seemed to reach inside the boy like a clever boxer and punch lightly at the core of his heart. Where they struck, the mud, churned by the heavy boots of the soldiers, geysered out into the air in cartloads, the ground shaking with the impact, the smoke thick and billowing. Where they flew, men shouted to take cover or lie flat or otherwise escape them. If the men were lucky, they escaped.

And some of the Japanese big guns were turned towards the village.

Imnuk took a deep breath.

'Quietly and carefully,' he said, clutching the boy's shoulder. 'Are you ready?'

He nodded and they crawled over the hilltop.

Crouching, nearly bent, they slithered down the slope, hiding behind the biggest pines they could find. But no one was looking in their direction. Through a break in the pines they saw a group of British break out from the trenches and dart towards a Japanese position at the base of Garrison Hill. They did not make it.

They reached the end of the treeline at the base of the hill. From here the land broke out into an irregular stony plain along a shallow creek. Along this, on the near bank, were a few abandoned huts.

'Do you see anyone?' Imnuk asked from behind a tree.

There was no movement to be seen.

'From here, we run straight across the creek, through those houses you see on the far side. Then we cross to Eastern Ridge. Do you hear?'

Eastern Ridge towered on the far side and at the moment looked far away. The boy nodded again, his head full of noise and chest full of choking air. He tightened the strap of the rifle on his back. The satchel was across his other shoulder.

'Now!' Imnuk pulled forward at his shirt. They dashed out from the cover of the trees, running over the stones. Stepping on a few rocks littering the creek, they ran forward. The butt of the rifle, which banged now and then against his upper thighs at the back, stopped him from taking long steps. He wanted to run faster, he wanted to finish this quickly.

They crossed the other bank and entered what had been Kohima town, a small collection of houses and shops. Some of these had been blown apart by shells, skeletons of houses standing draggled in the cold mud. The streets were a confusion of vehicle tracks and footsteps.

So, the British have brought in tanks too, thought Imnuk, reading the signs on the ground as they ran. I doubt it will help.

They ran past what must have been a shop of some kind, its tin roof blown away, its walls caving in, wood pillars cracked with bullet holes. H-A-K-R read the remainder of its sign, flapping by a piece of wire in the wind. The boy wondered what it meant.

They ran in a zigzag through the houses, not stepping into the street where they would be clearly seen.

That house looks familiar, the boy thought. I have seen it somewhere. The size, the design, the windows, even the broken glass display cupboards inside …

He read the painted sign.

Planters'. There is a Planters' Store here. That is, it used to be …

It was like seeing another old friend, hurt and wounded.

They heard a soft whistle. Imnuk clutched at the boy and pulled him to the side. 'Get down!' he hissed.

The shell struck a distance away on the other side of the street with a *krumpph*. It knocked them both off their feet, the hot blast of wind blowing through them and shaking loose a few more windowpanes. Another whistle and yet another followed. They landed further away. The Japanese were trying to bracket British positions. The next shells could be closer.

A machine gun opened up somewhere on the far side of the houses.

And a big gaping hole opened up in the floor of Gojen's mind. His instincts leaked out through this hole, and with them, rational thought. There was not a single thing he could remember any more. The sound of the shells filled this vacuum, rising and rising in volume, magnifying till the noise and heat were everywhere. His hands and feet felt disjointed, loose. Panic rose up from his legs in thick, inky waves. He wanted to keep crouching there, press his face and hands against the mud and wait for it to end.

Where am I? What am I doing here? What are these straps ... he thought, feeling behind him, the rifle hard and pressing against his back between him and the wood wall where they crouched. What happened?

Another shell landed, this time, it seemed, in a British trench. He heard the screams.

Imnuk was shaking him by the shoulders. He just looked stupidly at the hunter. Imnuk shook him harder.

'We have to run now!' the hunter said, half pulling, half dragging the boy along. He stepped across a street, turned quickly and crouched, pulling Gojen down with him. Around the corner they saw two British men, kneeling behind a pile of wood. One was middle-aged, in civilian clothes, but had the look of a soldier. The other was younger, larger and in uniform. This one held a pair of binoculars and was looking at the Japanese positions through it.

'They haven't seen us. We have a chance. Come on,' Imnuk said, pulling at Gojen's shirt again. The boy stood up reluctantly, shook his head, but the haze did not clear. His legs still felt loose. Imnuk dragged him forward again. They crossed the street.

The boy didn't know which way they were heading. He was confused and had lost all sense of direction. He followed Imnuk blindly, stumbling a little through the mud.

To one side was a jumble of objects, half-buried in the mud. They had familiar outlines ...

'Don't look!' said Imnuk, not wanting the boy to see the bodies.

138

They crossed another line of damaged houses and huts. Eastern Ridge loomed above them.

'It is clear from here,' said Imnuk, stopping. 'There is no place to hide. We have to run up as far as we can.' He looked at the boy searchingly.

Gojen nodded again. They set off. He tried to keep up with the hunter. This was another uneven patch of stones. The pines were closer. They dashed straight into the treeline and pushed up, up till they were panting with effort.

Imnuk slowed and stopped, put his hands on his knees and leaned forward, breathing hard. The boy flopped into the leafy ground on his side.

Imnuk started laughing. '*Ki*, you want to go back home?'

Gojen looked up at him blankly. There was a bitter feeling in his throat. His stomach was somersaulting rapidly. He spat to one side to get rid of the bitterness. He felt his hands and feet, adjusted the strap once more.

Then he looked at the hunter again and started laughing with him.

*

'I thought I saw something move,' said Kenneally, looking behind him.

'Perhaps they were native scouts. They can be very agile,' said the civilian, calmly.

He was always calm, Kenneally thought. If only all civilians were like this. But then, not all civilians were heroes of the First World War.

Charles Ridley Pawsey, formerly Captain, Worcestershire Regiment and Military Cross winner, was Deputy Commissioner, Naga Hills. When the Japanese spearhead crashed into Kohima, most civilian administrative staff, under advice, packed and left. Pawsey stayed. He lived in trenches with the troops defending his capital town while the battle reduced his official residence and the grounds around it to mud and ashes. British Intelligence was finding the fifty-year-old an invaluable adviser, for he knew as much about campaigns as he knew about the hills in this sector.

Kenneally looked behind him again. He had the heightened feeling, the rush soldiers get when they return to the field and his instincts told him to watch for any sudden movement, anywhere. He turned and focussed the binoculars at the fighting in the distance.

'Twenty-six years, and I find myself back in France,' Pawsey remarked. Kenneally could agree to that. It almost appeared as if the world had never moved away from fighting over inches, from trench to trench, a painful procession of light infantry facing their enemies at breathing distance, artillery keeping both sides cowed down.

Kenneally was thinking about Mori again. If the man was here, what an opportunity it was. If he could capture him alive, hold him up for trial, gather all the evidence and witnesses he was sure the Japanese officer had littered all over Asia. Kenneally was a passionate believer in the law and its processes, even though he admitted—now and then—that it was not sufficient. He believed in the laws which governed the conduct of men in uniform. He believed in the laws of his country.

Like any veteran soldier, he would have been the first to admit that war was a fundamentally *wrong* thing. Unlike civilian poets and aged politicians who glorified war, or even people who were pacifists because they were afraid of fighting, soldiers saw what war did to people like themselves. But if, because of reasons great or small, two countries reached a point where matters had to be resolved

140

through fighting, there were rules that governed this too. Trained men met trained men on a plain or a hillside or a desert or the sea and duelled with each other. Sometimes they met in towns and this was not good. But they had training and discipline. Armed men did *not* wage war against civilians, against the old and the very young, against the truly innocent. People like Mori could not be called soldiers. Perhaps they couldn't even be called humans.

But there were other, more urgent matters that occupied Kenneally's attention at the moment. A day earlier, on 20 April, at about six in the morning, Colonel Richards, the very weary commander of Kohima's main garrison, had handed over command to the troops which had arrived to relieve him. But that was a merely symbolic lifting of the siege. The Japanese were dug in, strong as ever, and they were not ready to turn around and leave just yet.

All the advances in military technology had come to nothing here. Kenneally watched through the lenses as a Royal Armoured Corps tank rumbled up an incline, the tank looking heavy and purposeful. It was on its way to help the Royal Welch Fusiliers around Garrison Hill.

Its treads dug into the mud, churned it some more and it came to a stop, turret inclined at a difficult angle. The tank just stood half-buried in the mud, looking like a puzzled elephant. Kenneally thought, And there goes armoured warfare. Sooner or later, the tank would lose a tread or bang against a tree and its commander would have to evacuate. This ridge was where all the fancy theories ended.

'Lt Colonel, how are we placed at the moment, artillery-wise?' Pawsey asked, taking the binoculars and looking.

'Sir,' the Intelligence man said, for though Pawsey had been a Captain, he outranked Kenneally as an administrator. 'We are bringing in the howitzers. If it weren't for road conditions, it would be quicker.'

'Ah, the weather again. What kind?' He meant, what kind of howitzers: towed guns.

'3.7 inchers. Uncle Bill says we should get two dozen of them, perhaps more.'

'What else? We will need a lot of heavy equipment.'

'Twenty-five-pounder field guns, perhaps forty of those, if not more. There might be a few 5.5 inch medium artillery pieces as well.'

'How soon, do you think?'

'If the weather holds, late tonight, maybe by dawn tomorrow. The heavy equipment is more difficult to transport on these roads. You know what happens to vehicles here when it rains.'

'This is the right time for a counter-offensive. You know that. We have to seize the initiative while we have it.'

Pawsey and Kenneally had gone over each reported location of Japanese troops on the map. Their plan was a swift, large attack from the direction of Garrison Hill and IGH Spur, aimed at the large mass of enemy forces south of these positions and west of Imphal Road. But they needed more artillery fire to support their infantry's advance.

'Sir, I assure you, with the guns promised, we will be in place for a counter-attack in ... two days at the most. It will not be later than that.'

The Deputy Commissioner looked up at the clouds which never seemed to lift from Kohima Ridge. 'If the weather holds and if the Japanese do not surprise us. As Burns says: the best-laid plans of mice and men ...'

13

The other members of the group joined them, singly and in groups, through the evening. The Angami led them straight up the Eastern Ridge. The incline was only a little less than perpendicular at this point. Climbing was difficult. The ridge widened and became a gradual slope on its further, eastern side, but their route lay straight southward. Far beneath, Imphal Road undulated on its way south into the plains of Manipur. Around it, the battle continued.

Their host called for a halt on a wide ledge of stone much into the night. They could not risk lighting a fire, so they chewed more pork strips and washed them down with water.

Gojen was feeling like he had crossed the pain barrier while running cross-country: a point during a long-distance run when the aching joints and throbbing limbs and stitches in the stomach suddenly faded away and the body was running like a machine, mechanically and onward. He felt, if not fresh, at least alert and raring to go. All his senses were in high gear and he was beginning to feel the thrill of the hunt. This contrasted in strange ways with his usual willingness to lie still.

Meren and the Angami were having a hushed discussion on ways and means. The latter was arguing that they could not risk crossing Imphal Road into Japanese lines without being certain of where their quarry was.

Capturing a Japanese soldier and questioning him thoroughly was the simplest idea, but none of them knew the language. A better idea, the mission leaders thought, would be to send scouts through the lines up the hill where Japanese officers were supposed to be.

The matter was still not solved to everyone's satisfaction when they rested for the night on the ledge.

Another day's march began early. They made their way across a little-known trail beneath the skyline of the ridge, hidden by pines from unknown watchers below.

'Look,' said Imnuk, pointing at a mountain to the south-west, its top wreathed with clouds. 'Japfu Peak.' The boy looked at the second-highest peak in the Naga Hills and at the mist which seemed to flow down from it to the dwarfed ridges around its base.

The trail ended nearly parallel with Garrison Hill to their west. From here they climbed carefully through a pile of big rocks which looked ready to slide down the ridge on to the road. Their path carried them downhill. They could see Japanese trenches and gun nests surrounding the defenders. It was a risk if the group was seen by Japanese soldiers, but there was no way to avoid it. They halted in a thick grove of pines. Every step from here to the south would have to be taken with care.

But the dawn brought another peril, this time from above. They heard a low buzzing noise in the distance, far above the clouds.

'Under the trees and stay still!' the Angami shouted. They separated and ran, crouching, towards the thickness of the trees. Gojen and Imnuk sprinted to a clump of bushes downhill, lay prone and curled up. The hunter pointed to the northern sky, through gaps in the pines.

'Keep watching,' he said.

Four aircraft broke through the cloudbank which seemed to have dropped even lower during the night. They were not flying in a line, or a square or any formation the boy could remember. They just made a zigzag pattern: one plane in the lead, another to its right and behind, the other behind the second and to its left. They dived in unison, keeping a constant distance.

These were big planes, two propellers to a wing, slower, heavier than the fighters.

'Bombers?' asked the boy, fascinated. But Imnuk shook his head.

Lower they dived and lower. Guns opened up. These sounded different; the gunfire made a hollow echoing noise. He watched the shells flower in the sky.

'Anti-aircraft,' explained Imnuk.

The planes arrested their dive. Small dots fell from them and disappeared far away somewhere on the ground. The planes roared nearer but were not hit. The formation pointed its nose skyward and vanished into the clouds.

'They can't bomb the Japani, but they drop supplies to the Ingraz all over the place. Wait,' he said to Gojen, who was about to get up. 'They usually return once more before going back to the plains. Do you see any Ingraz soldiers nearby?'

The boy shook his head.

'Then, if they see us, will they bomb us or not?'

Gojen considered this, nodded and crouched once more. But the planes did not return.

'Back to the clearing, boy,' Imnuk said, picking up his crossbow from the ground.

'Will they decide on a plan soon?'

'Who knows? Sending scouts at night is a good idea, I think. But there are so many Japani in the south, you wouldn't believe. Where are you going?'

Gojen was making his way further downhill. 'I think one of the packs fell somewhere ahead.'

'Then it fell on Imphal Road, or maybe on the heads of some Japani patrol. They sometimes get more supplies than the Ingraz do. Come up.'

'There is nothing to do there except listen to Meren and the Angami arguing. If I find a pack it will be good, won't it?'

'Gojen, if you find a pack, you stand in the middle of Imphal Road and shout to the Japani brothers, all right?' Imnuk laughed.

'I will be quiet,' said the boy and moved downhill.

The hill rolled down in nearly vertical walls. Sliding would have been easier but noisy, so the boy dug his heels into the ground and walked softly over the pine needles. Beyond the trees he could see Imphal Road. He listened carefully, but there was no noise of men talking. The stretch of road was empty as far as he could see.

He sat down at the base of a tree, carefully stretched his legs out and checked all the sides. There was no one. The fighting was far away. And wherever the pack had dropped, it definitely hadn't landed where he could see it.

The Eastern Ridge at this point seemed to approach a hill on the opposite side. The road, from what he could see, disappeared through a narrow gap between the two hills.

This is what Kohima must have looked like before the battle began, he thought, looking at the view through the pines. Tall green trees with creepers, shrubs, round green stones and thin grass covering the slopes. He traced the slope to its peak and back again. Then he thought quickly, in a rush, almost.

Round stones? He remembered each part of the vegetation on these hills, for the hunter learns to look for the unusual, the not-in-place, the part that does not fit. Yet he did not remember a single place anywhere else which had these round green stones. Why should this hill be any different? He traced the slope back downhill. There they were. Now they looked like some kind of fruit. But the size meant they must be *large* fruits. How strange. There were very, very few things in nature which were perfectly geometrical, angular or spherical.

Then he tried to focus through the shade of the trees and the fruit-stones became semicircles of green and *polished* semicircles of green and became helmets on the heads of ten soldiers climbing slowly up the slope. He sat up and hid behind a tree from where he looked out. There they went, climbing up that hill with effort. He could just see the outline of the guns and packs on their backs. Japani soldiers.

Some patrol, he thought, trying to remember the British map. There were many patrols up and down this road, but he didn't know they climbed the hills too. He looked around to make sure there was no one climbing *his* hill. But there were only those ten. They advanced upward slowly, keeping beneath the skyline, and disappeared over the top.

They must be climbing down the other side to their trenches. The map, if he remembered correctly, did not say anything about Japanese positions here, did it? So the Angami's maps were useless, unless he had understood everything wrong. He retraced the path of their ascent, working his eyes down through the trees. He saw movement.

Slowly, keeping his eyes fixed on the spot, he inched

around the tree and pushed himself downhill and closer till he was almost at the edge of the slope. This was the furthest he could go. Sheltering behind another tree, he looked again.

Men were moving. One, two. Two men were standing up, no, they were leaning against the hillside, next to a ... He saw a head and shoulders emerge from the ground. Another man. A black block of some kind of weapon at the spot.

A trench. What was the word for it? A nest. A machine gun nest.

Further ahead, he saw another outline: this one bigger, bulkier. Perhaps a mortar, he thought. Still further, another outline, similar to the first one. The hill was full of big guns and Japanese.

He sat back, his heart racing. The Japanese had guns all along the road. The hill down the road where Japanese officers were supposed to be must be infinitely better guarded. What chance did they have?

His first instinct was to run straight up the hill and shout out his find, but he checked himself. He had to make sure of what he had seen. He looked around the tree once more. Yes, there were the men and there were the guns.

Several thoughts struck him at once. Edging away from the slope, he pushed uphill.

They were *still* debating over the map when he found them in the clearing. Imnuk caught his look and walked over from where he sat with his crossbow.

Gojen walked up to where Meren and the Angami sat on a rock.

'What is this hill?' he asked, pointing at the map and looking at the Angami.

'This one?' their host said. 'Ingraz call it Kuki Picquet. It is just a small hill, not important.'

'There are Japani on the hill.'

The Angami looked at him and tried his best to be patient. 'Rajkhowa, we are *behind* Japani lines. So, yes, there are Japani everywhere. It is our good fortune there are no Japani *here*. Now, please take your hand away from the map.'

'What is on the other side of that hill?'

Meren could see he was driving at something, but not what he was driving at. 'You went down there?' Meren asked him, looking at Imnuk accusingly.

'I went down a short distance to see if the planes dropped something around there. But you tell me, what is on the other side of the hill?'

'Why?'

'Because I saw Japani soldiers climbing up it and they did not return.'

'There is nothing on the other side. Look,' said the Angami, wanting this discussion to end. 'On this map it looks like the west side of this hill of yours is full of Japani. But the west slope is a steep drop straight to its base. The hill just falls down. So there are no soldiers on the western slope, only at its base. The soldiers you saw must have been a patrol.'

Gojen counted off on his fingers. 'I saw two machine guns and a mortar on its eastern slope and I saw ten men go up the hill and disappear.'

But after 'mortar' everybody was paying attention.

'You saw a mortar?' the Angami asked suspiciously. 'How would you know a mor—' but Meren waved him to be quiet.

The boy had an idea, so the first thing he thought about was a pencil and a piece of paper, realised there was none, looked for a stick to draw on the ground, found the ground full of stones and flung up his hands in despair. He took a few small pebbles in his hand.

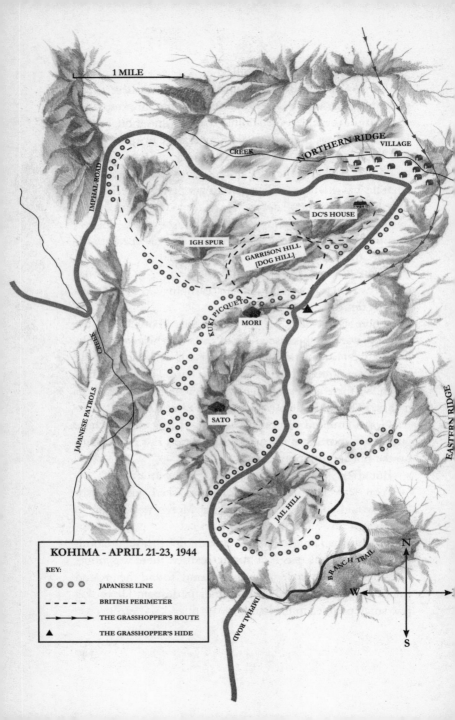

KOHIMA – APRIL 21-23, 1944

KEY:

⊙ ⊙ ⊙ ⊙   JAPANESE LINE

– – – – –   BRITISH PERIMETER

→ → → →   THE GRASSHOPPER'S ROUTE

▲   THE GRASSHOPPER'S HIDE

'This is the hill,' he said, placing a large stone on the ground. 'On its side, there are three nests. I saw all three and there are men inside them. There are two machine guns and a mortar. Now,' he said, standing up and wiping his hands on his shorts, 'tell me this: do the Japani have big guns *inside* their lines?'

The Angami shrugged. 'They could have.'

'They have guns facing inside and not toward the British? They put their guns in a place from where they can't fire at the British? Why would they do that?'

The Angami, despite appearances, was listening with interest.

Gojen pointed at the map again. 'There is only one way up that hill. On this path, there are three big guns and soldiers. What does it tell you?'

Imnuk said, in his careful, reasoning voice: 'The guns are not looking at the Ingraz. They are looking *away* from the fight. There is something behind their back, up the hill. They are protecting it.'

'What is up the hill?' Meren asked the Angami.

The latter curled his lips, still unwilling to concede that the plainsman had a point. 'The hilltop is round. I think there is a depression there, beneath the trees. It is wider than this,' he pointed around himself at the clearing. 'They could have guns there to fire at the Ingraz to the west. But ... no, it isn't possible.'

'Why?'

'Because the slope is too steep to carry heavy guns up there. And it is far from Ingraz lines, so if the planes find out about the guns they will bomb them.'

'What do you think?' Meren asked the boy.

'I don't know, but why would the Japanese put three big guns in a place where there is no fighting? I think they are

151

there to protect the only route to the hilltop, which means there is something important up there. Or someone,' he added meaningfully.

The Angami said with a short laugh, 'What, you think Mori is up there?'

'Or somebody else. Meren, do you remember what the British officer had written. This man is some kind of observer. *He will not be where we expect him to be*, the letter said. Remember? It could be possible.'

'You are seeing Mori everywhere,' said the Angami. 'There is no reason why he should not be with the rest of their senior officers, that way.' He pointed south.

'But there is something important on the hilltop. Can you explain this otherwise?' Gojen asked, kicking at the three stones at his feet. They rolled off down the slope.

'We are not here to explain. We move south now.'

The boy looked at Meren. 'I want to take a closer look at these nests. You promised me I was here to observe and use my head. I am going back downhill and I will find out what this is. I need some time.'

Everything the boy said seemed to point at there being something on the hilltop. The hill was valuable for the Japani, that was certain. And there was hardly anything to lose if Gojen took a look, was there? From a safe place, of course. And if he did find out what was going on there, perhaps it could help.

'We have a lot of time and many things to decide. We cannot make a move in daylight. The Japani are not going anywhere today. Neither are the Ingraz and nor are we. You come back as soon as you are sure of what you see. And don't go any closer than necessary.'

Imnuk tried to follow behind him, but Gojen waved him

off and walked downhill, aware of the eyes on him. 'You promised him *what*?' the Angami asked but Meren waved away the question wearily and asked him if they could now decide how to proceed south and find Mori.

*

Sato wished he was younger. Climbing up and down hills was not comfortable for his knees. But he had made his weary way to Mori's post, breathing heavily.

'General,' Mori had said, not even bothering to bow at the senior officer in his bunker. 'I have good news for you. I have prepared a plan of attack. From our positions at the western base of this hill and positions near your hill,' he pointed on the map, 'our men will move north in a large wave, through the British positions on Garrison Hill and IGH Spur, across the east-west section of Imphal Road. We will shut down the British advance before it even begins. I have given orders to the men to begin moving slowly forward and prepare for the attack.'

'And how, Colonel, will this attack succeed when others did not?'

'We will attack at precisely 10 p.m. tomorrow night. Fresh artillery supplies will reach us today, headquarters says. With those, we will mount an all-out offensive.'

'At night?' The losses would be huge.

'The British will not expect it, or our artillery firepower. It is a foolproof plan, General. Headquarters has agreed to it.'

A foolproof plan indeed, thought Sato. 'I will discuss this with my other officers before I agree, Colonel. I do not approve of it.'

Mori did not bother to reply.

14

It took him longer than he expected, inching down the hillside. Beneath him and to his right, he found a small spur of the hillside jutting out in a triangular shape, its base far below. At this point, Imphal Road curved around the base. He made his way to this spur, moving from the cover of one tree to another, hoping nobody had binoculars in those nests. At the base of the hill, he saw, trees along a certain distance had been cut, perhaps by Japanese soldiers who needed the wood for their trenches and bunkers and also to make sure there was no place for a small ambush group to hide and wait for patrols along Imphal Road.

From the edge of the trees, the ground was clear to the embankment along which Imphal Road ran. There was another embankment on the other side of the road too. This might have been made to prevent rainwater from filling up the road. Out here, he reflected, there seemed to be reasons for everything.

On the spur, and a short distance from the edge of the hillside, he found what he was looking for: a hollow which could have been where the roots of a pine had dug into the earth before the tree had fallen down long ago, though no sign of it remained. It was a shallow depression in the ground, just the right length, filled with grass, leaves and pine needles.

He crouched, cleared some of them away, decided there were no nests of crawling insects underneath, unrolled the blanket and covered it with leaves. It was a warm blanket and he needed the warmth, but it was also bright red. He lay prone in the depression, legs stretched behind him, comfortable in a familiar position, for he might be here a long time. His rifle lay at his side with the satchel.

He was. He lay there and watched for nearly eleven hours, fixing his eyes on the nests across the road, occasionally chewing on pork strips or drinking water, hardly moving at all, for who knew if those soldiers had binoculars?

Clouds covered the sky from end to end. Mist drifted in small patches down from Japfü. The mountain breeze came and chilled him underneath his shirt—the cold dampness of the ground working its way in as well. From time to time, he flexed his fingers, elbows and knees which would be the first to cramp in this cold-soaked motionlessness. Hunger came in a while, as it always did particularly when he had to wait, but he was used to small rations in the field. He tried not to think of the past and focus on the here and now. It struck him that this could be a waste of time and he wasn't making friends if he slowed the group's march.

But it still did not make sense.

Kenneally had written that Mori was always on guard against attempts on his life. Why otherwise would there be soldiers and big guns on the one side of a hill that did not face the enemy at all? Ever since the day he had got Kenneally's letter, Gojen had pictured Mori as a kind of fearful, bullying man constantly on watch against just the kind of people stalking him today.

Could such a man be guarded by a position like this?

Gojen did not know. He only knew of creatures which were so fearful of the world that they crept into burrows in the ground and tried to protect themselves at all times, even when their known predators were very few.

The soldiers in the nests seemed an impatient lot. One or the other would constantly be coming out and stretching his legs. He estimated the distance between them. The two machine guns were on each corner, the mortar in the middle and there was a large distance between them. In fact, he thought, the machine guns probably did not see each other, but all three covered the hill, the road and his hill too.

At midday, the sun seemed to be trying to appear but changed its mind. Two hours later, someone else appeared. There was a rustling of leaves behind him and Imnuk crawled into the hollow. The rustling had been on purpose, a friendly warning.

'Are they talking about me back there?' Gojen asked, his eyes still on the opposite hill.

'No. Don't worry. They think you made a good find, whatever it is. This is a nice hiding place you found. It even slopes like your range at home. Have you seen anything?'

'The soldiers came down the hill and are sitting around the nests. Look, just behind the trees.'

'They came back?'

The boy nodded. 'Or,' he said reasonably, 'ten other soldiers.'

Imnuk laughed quietly. 'How many soldiers do you imagine are on the hilltop? They go up, others come down ...'

'The mortar nest has a radio.'

'A radio? Where? Did you see it?' Imnuk tried to look.

'One of the men stood up when the soldiers came down. He was saying something into his hand. I think there was a wire leading into the nest ...'

'You can't see a *wire* from here, Gojen.'

'They were all gathered around the mortar. The man was holding his hand up to his mouth, like he was holding a speaker. It looked like they were listening. Then, after some time, some Japanese came up the road and climbed the hill. There must have been a senior officer with them, because the men climbed out of the nests and bowed.' He wished he had binoculars too, but it would have been impossible for anyone to steal a pair from the British.

It was the old game. He saw what he saw, except the tiny parts which explain the whole story in an instant, and these he had to guess. Two soldiers standing next to each other, talking. From the way they stood, the way they listened or replied, the gestures they made to each other, he had to guess what was being said. It was the method of observation that lies beyond lip-reading.

It was dull. Some Japanese officer had struck on the brilliant idea of posting men and guns here for whatever reason and that was that.

At 4 p.m., sipping from the goatskin water bag and listening to Imnuk guessing that there was a Japanese flying tank division and fifty herds of goats on the hilltop, the boy's wait was rewarded.

*

Mori accompanied Sato downhill, explaining once more why the plan just could not fail. Couldn't the General see he was so happy with the plan he was even walking his guest out? But Sato had made up his mind to think about it and reply later and could not be convinced otherwise.

Superior Private Isoya inside the machine gun pit was thinking of home, as he often did. He saw the General and the Colonel coming downhill and tried to climb out on time.

'No, no,' said Sato, motioning him not to bother. 'How is everything?'

'It is good, General-*san*,' said Isoya, making an incomplete bow from inside the pit.

'You are getting your rations on time?' Sato asked.

'Of course they are, General,' said Mori, taking the senior officer's elbow. Sato brushed his hand aside. 'Mori, we cannot take unnecessary risks at this stage. An attack at night is nearly impossible. We will end up shooting at one another.'

'General, the plan, as I said, is foolproof. We are to go ahead. You only have to decide whether you approve of it or not, but in either event, we attack tomorrow.'

'In that case, I want some of the men you have posted here. We will need as many as we can afford. And we need the mortar.'

'That is not possible, General.'

'Mori,' said Sato angrily. 'You will order half your men to report to my post by this evening and you will send the mortar with them. That is an order.'

Sato is trying to leave me exposed, thought Mori, but he wanted to appear friendly. Sato could still upset his plans. 'Fine, General. You will have half the men from this post, but I cannot release the mortar unless you ask headquarters directly for it.'

And Sato had to be content with that.

*

They stood there, the shorter, older Japanese and the taller one, under the pines near the nests. Gojen crunched up his eyes and stared hard. The taller man rested his weight on one leg, the other bent a little, hands at his waist. He was talking with the shorter, older officer. The latter could be a senior officer, but it did not seem likely. The younger man's gestures and posture were like those people kept for their subordinates.

But Gojen saw the same way of standing, the same approximate size from what he remembered of the photograph, the same way of looking down, if only he had binoculars, if only there was more sunlight …

Then the man brought his hands down from his waist. The boy saw a thin line at the belt of the Japanese.

'Imnuk,' he whispered, his hand clutching the barrel of the rifle tight and pulling it toward himself. 'Do you see that man?'

'Which one?'

'The tall one. Look at his waist. Is that a knife?'

'Where?'

'There. Look, at his waist. There is a black line on it down nearly to his knees.'

Imnuk had good eyes too.

'It could be …' he said, unsure. 'But it doesn't mean anything. Every Japanese officer carries a sword. Some of them wear it everywhere.'

'This one looks smaller than their usual swords, just like the English said it would. He is the right height and right shape.'

'Good. Can you see his shoulder boards too?' Imnuk joked.

'Collar.'

'Hmm?'

'Japanese soldiers' rank symbols are on their collars, not shoulders like the British.'

'I know. You still can't see him clearly enough to be sure.'

'Imnuk, when you went into the trees after the wild pig, how did you know where it would be?'

'Simple. I knew all about it. I knew how big it was, how it moved, what noises it made when it moved and which places it would be hiding in.'

'Imnuk, I have thought only of Mori since the British sent me the photograph. That Japanese there: that is Mori.'

'And you know what the Angami will say? He will say that *you* see Mori everywhere.'

'What do you say?'

'I say my eyes are getting old and you should keep looking at whoever he is.'

He watched the officer walk through the shade of the pines, up the hillside, along the same route the soldiers had climbed earlier, the boy's eyes following every step. Further up climbed the Japanese. Then he made his mistake.

At the top of the hill, too far for his features to be seen clearly but near enough for a calculated estimation, the Japanese showed up against the skyline, the one thing a hunter never does in the hills. There was still no sunlight, but the man stood distinctly silhouetted under the pines, looking to the south where the other officer had gone down the road.

And Gojen, looking long and hard at the silhouette, the photograph and Kenneally's information running in his mind, was certain.

'It is Mori.' *There you are, Japanese.*

Imnuk did not reply.

They stayed in their hiding place. Two hours later, another roar came from the clouds and a second RAF sortie followed, but this time the planes did not drop any supplies.

160

'Don't the Japanese ever hit the planes?' the boy asked.

Imnuk laughed. 'They haven't hit a plane here yet. Who knows why? But don't worry about the pilots. Meren tells me during the Great War in France, they had much smaller planes made of cloth or something. If the planes were hit, the pilots did not have a way out. They would try to land the planes or crash in them. Flying was a horrible thing to do. Now they have parachutes.'

Soon after the sortie, things started happening that made both the watchers sit up and take notice. A line of men appeared on the hilltop and snaked down to the gun nests. From here they marched downhill to Imphal Road, making Gojen and Imnuk crouch lower in the hollow.

'Twenty, twenty-five, thirty,' Imnuk counted. After sixty he gave up. 'How many are on the hilltop, Gojen? What have you found for us?'

About ninety men (and they looked like a lot to the watchers) marched down Imphal Road. It was very strange to see, but stranger thoughts were beginning to occur to the boy watching them.

Other things were happening at the nests.

At dusk, the hunter and the boy rejoined their group.

'Somewhere on the hilltop is Mori. I don't know what they have there, but it is him.'

'Imnuk?' the Angami asked, thinking, if the boy is correct ...

'It is Mori,' said the hunter quietly. Gojen tried not to look at him. 'I am certain and the boy is even more certain. It is the man.'

They returned to Gojen's hollow downhill, Meren and the Angami with them. It was night but lit with gun flashes in the distance. They could just barely see the three gun nests.

'There are many soldiers on the hilltop,' Imnuk said, telling the two Nagas about the marching men. 'If there were ninety men there, there would be many, many more.'

'Not many,' their host remarked, 'maybe another ninety. The top of the hill is not very wide and they will probably have trenches and a bunker of some kind. That is how they make their hiding places. They can't have much space for many men.'

'Can it be seen by the planes?' Imnuk asked.

'Things look different from the air,' Meren said, who knew of such things. 'If they have left the trees intact the planes will not see anything.'

'Imnuk,' said the Angami, 'I trust your judgment. If you say you saw the man, it could be possible. We could even manage against ninety or a hundred men if we surprised them. But I will not risk the lives of my men against such a position when we are not completely sure if we will succeed. Look at the hill.'

It was a steep hillside with vertical pines and sparse undergrowth. From its base, which had been cleared, a gentle slope rose three-quarters of the way to the top. It was the only way uphill.

At the upper end of this slope were the three big guns.

'I can get twenty men or so from the scout camp in the north. Guns are not a problem. But see this ...' said the Angami, pointing to the base of their hill. He pointed at the cleared trees, the stretch of Imphal Road, the cleared base of the opposite hill. 'There is no cover. Even at night, if we try to run across, we will be seen by the mortar and machine guns. Even if some of us reach the trees on that side, there will be more soldiers at the nests by the time we get there. You said they have a radio in the mortar pit, didn't you? It is

162

there for just such an attack. No, if it is Mori, he has been very clever. We can't take the hill.'

'We can,' said Gojen and the three Nagas looked at him.

'We can,' he said again, slowly, calmly. Once again, he was on the hunt and had recovered his initiative. Once again he had seen the land and the prey and looked at the situation with the hunter's eye. Over the day's watch, he had thought long and hard over what he must do and although some questions remained unresolved, he had dealt with the major ones.

'Imnuk, tell them what we saw at dusk,' he asked.

'Meren,' said the hunter, 'there are ten soldiers in the trees behind the nests, at all times. They change twice a day, as do the gun nests, but at different times. The big gun crew changed at midday, so maybe they will change again at midnight, which means they have twelve-hour shifts. The soldiers change at dawn and dusk. But there is a difference.'

'Meren,' said the boy. 'The ten soldiers go uphill and others return in their place, carrying food, I think. Between when the soldiers leave and others return, there are only the gun crews in the nests. But this is only for a short while—I think about a quarter of an hour.'

'It doesn't make a difference,' said the Angami. 'The gun crews will still be there, won't they? One mortar shell will finish us.'

'There are five men in the nests,' the boy said, his eyes on the other hill. 'Two men with the mortar, two with the machine gun on our right and one with the machine gun in the left. The mortar pit is the one with the radio. In the time between when the ten soldiers leave and others return, if we stop them from calling the hilltop, go uphill and attack the hilltop before they are warned …'

'How do we do that?' the Angami was asking himself. 'We don't have artillery, do we? How do we blow up the guns? The men on the hilltop will hear us even if we had the explosives to do it.'

'We don't need artillery,' said the boy, thinking of what Imnuk had said earlier in the day. *This hollow looks like your range at home.* 'We don't need to hit the guns. We need to hit the gunners.'

'All at once? With rifles? From where, from this hill?' the Angami scoffed. 'It is too far and we can't get any closer safely. It can't be done.'

'I can,' said the boy evenly and held up his hand before Meren could say anything. 'The gun crews on the right and left can't see each other very well, but you can see all of them clearly from here. I can take them quickly, one after the other...'

'No, you won't,' said Meren angrily. 'Imnuk, it seems the artillery fire back in the village has knocked his brains loose. Does he even know what he is saying?'

Imnuk just spread his hands in the near-darkness to show his helplessness, thinking: if all this talk had been leading up to this, why didn't I stop it before it began?

'This is not your home, Gojen. This is not about your marksmanship. You will not cross this line. This is not your work and you *will* not do it,' Meren said.

'Fine,' said the boy. 'I just gave you my idea. If anyone else can do it, it is fine. Can anyone?'

But they looked at the hill and what they could see of the nests and each one was thinking: it is a good plan. It can be done that way. But there is no one to do it.

'So it won't be done. We don't even know if we will go up and find the right man,' the Angami said, but he was thinking, it just *could* be Mori.

'All right. But if I have been right about everything I have seen, just wait and watch. The gun crews will change at midnight. Will that convince you?' the boy asked.

And so it happened.

A little past midnight, Meren sat by himself uphill from the boy's hiding place, looking at what he could see of the enemy. The last of the soldiers from the gun nests had disappeared over the hill. In his heart he was sure the boy had found Mori. He trusted the boy like his son. He had loved both of them, Gojen and Uti. He could not let the boy cross this final line. What would he think of himself afterwards if he allowed it?

It was ironic: Shilukaba had given him command. He was supposed to take decisions. Yet, here he found himself, facing a situation where the only solution was one he did not want to face. But what else could he do? In the face of such reasoned conviction that they had found the man they were hunting, could he just drop everything and move on?

He looked at the distant gun nests and wished none of this had happened. But it had and he could not change anything. If only there was someone else to make the decision. But there was none.

'We will go ahead,' he told the Angami. 'Do you trust me?'

The Angami nodded.

*

Sato's officers agreed to a man that Mori's plan would throw their soldiers into a needless fight whose outcome was so uncertain the plan should not have been approved at all. But they had run up against the distant brick wall called 15th Imperial Japanese Army Headquarters.

'What can we do, Shigesaburo-*san*,' Sato asked of Lt Gen. Miyazaki. 'It is out of our hands. We can only sit here and listen to whatever Mori chooses to tell us, when he chooses to.'

'Sato-*san*, when will the attack go ahead?'

'Ten tonight, he says. It is out of our hands.'

*

By early dawn, three men were sent back to the British Naga Scouts camp. Whispered discussions took place and more than twenty grim men walked out in small groups to Eastern Ridge carrying 'borrowed' British guns. It was not difficult.

Gojen was glad Imnuk did not leave him alone in the hollow—he was exhausted battling Uti inside his head. They watched and watched, without a word, as the crews and soldiers changed again precisely on schedule.

The boy had, slowly and soundlessly, built up a pile of earth, stones and pine needles in front of him, the pile densely packed. On this he was resting the rifle and his forearms.

'Imnuk, don't try to stop me now.'

The hunter had opened his mouth to say something but closed it, hearing new tones in his student's voice.

'No,' said Imnuk. 'I was only going to say Meren was right. You knocked your head loose back in Kohima town.'

Gojen did not hear him, his eyes fixed on the gun nests, estimating their distances from each other, from him, what he could see of the gun crew. Calculations were tumbling around in his head.

'Meren does not like this.'

'Does he have a better idea?' asked the boy, turning his head to look at Imnuk.

'This is not what we wanted,' said Imnuk softly.

I did not want Uti to die either, the boy thought, and he is in his grave at Mokokchung and I haven't even visited it yet. I did not want anything that happened after it.

Midday brought more mist along Imphal Road.

'A little mist should help us,' said Gojen, chewing on pork strips and trying to ignore the jolts of hot current in his stomach he always felt during moments of high tension or while running. It was called something, he knew. But not a lot of mist.

Dusk approached. The soldiers across the road made ready to go uphill. Meren came down softly behind the hollow and called Imnuk. They left the boy who returned to whatever thoughts he was having. Who could guess?

'Imnuk …' said Meren as they made their way downhill where the men were gathering beneath the pines at the base, a short distance from where the trees had been cleared.

'I know,' said Imnuk. 'Don't talk about it now.'

The Angami passed Meren and asked him: 'You are sure this will work? Is he that good with a rifle?' But Meren was loading a magazine to his Sten and did not answer. He looked angry.

Imnuk unbuttoned and took off his shirt and picked up his crossbow and Sten. Arrowhead tattoos ran over his chest and back. On his chest was a tattoo of two broad leaves.

'Look,' said someone, in the light-but-heavy voice of men about to go into a fight. 'Imnuk has found his magic leaves again.'

But Imnuk, who had taken off his shirt because he wanted to go into battle the old way, tattoos gleaming, did not say a word. He checked his crossbow and the Sten and because there was still some time left, he checked his weapons again, trying not to think of his little brother on the hillside above him.

*

'Mr Pawsey,' said Kenneally. 'We are ready to begin.'

167

Uncle Bill had not let his men down. The new big guns had arrived and were being hauled into position to begin bombing the Japanese.

'Good, Lt Colonel. I see the troops are in place too. When do you think will be a good time?'

'I could say "now",' said Kenneally with a smile, 'but midnight sounds fine.'

'Midnight, then.'

15

Look at you now, said Uti, laughing in his ear. *Here you are, damp and itching, on a cold hillside, looking at the mist and five men, trying to ignore a ghost. And you told me you were going to school far away to study with the Ingraz.*

Look at you now. There is no one else. There is only you and the rifle you have brought on your back, up and down over the hills and ravines, through the mud and the shells and the broken houses, through the wind and the rain.

There is no one else watching you now. KC is not here, encouraging you with a proud gleam in his old eyes. Your father is not here, wanting to know what you have learnt in school, the two of you circling around each other. Your mother is not here to tell you that you look thin because the school does not feed you as well as she does. Your grandmother is not here either, suspicious about what you might soon do. Shilukaba is not here with his wisdom. Meren, Imnuk, they are down there on the slope somewhere. I am here, but I don't count.

No one is coming to tell you to get up and brush the mud and leaves off your hands and face. No one will call you to come back home, eat your fill and get into a warm soft bed and not worry about anything because it was only a game and now it is over. There is only you, and you have to finish it.

What was it called? He thought, his hands locking into the familiar position on the bank of leaves, the position his body remembered automatically from countless hours at the range and in the swamps and forest. There was a phrase he had heard from someone. Bartlett? KC? Someone who read a lot of big books with answers to many things.

What was it called? 'The "something" of the actual.' It was a phrase, he recalled, his right palm curved around the bolt, pulling it back. It was a phrase that was supposed to stand for the moment when things *happened* in the big world. It was a stage on which hard men acted out their parts in a hard situation, when men moved things and circumstances and got stuff done, even though it might seem that the men were being moved by circumstances themselves.

The something … Pan? Sieve? Cauldron? That was a big word. It was a cooking pot of some kind, wasn't it? The cauldron of the actual? The anvil? That sounded right. 'The anvil of the actual.' It was true here, at least, he thought, his ears hammered again and again by the big guns firing all over the ridge. But it was not the right phrase.

He shook his head to get rid of pans and phrases he could not recall, aligned his rifle over the mound of leaves and stones, and looked down the sights.

The two men at the mortar nest were talking to each other. It was too far away to see their faces clearly, but one was gesturing and the other was shaking his head. What were they talking about? Don't think of it, he told himself, remembering the Japanese soldiers climbing up the hill that morning long ago. You can see them. They can't see you. They don't know what is about to happen. Don't think of it. Think, if it helps, of the cold inside since you got off the boat. Why are you here? Do you remember?

Looking down the sights, his estimation was more precise than before: 260 yards, maybe a fraction less. It was just within the maximum point-blank range of his rifle. Would it make a big difference? Within this distance and at sea level, the rifle fired exactly as aimed with almost no variation in the flight path of the bullet. But beyond ...

He was ... how much, 3,290 feet up? That would be about 1,000 metres above sea level. Perhaps. Why am I thinking about useless conversions now? How much difference will the altitude make? There was no wind at all, the sound of shells bursting clear in his ears, somewhat muted by the mist. Maybe the bullet would drop less than an inch. He was firing at the very edge of the rifle's precision capacity and well beyond any targets he had aimed at before, creature or cardboard. He could barely see the features on their faces. They had been at the village. Maybe these were the soldiers who'd actually killed Uti. Who could say? But at the moment he had only one reason.

It had to be done.

You are not going to make a mistake now, are you, Fat Boy? Uti whispered at his side.

If you can't help but can only make comments, why don't you let me do this now and talk later? the boy whispered back.

He chambered the round, aiming at the man in the mortar nest, just the upper body visible, looking away into the distance. He squeezed his eyes shut; his hands tight and locked over the mound. He opened his eyes and settled into the position, feet spread a little behind him, knees pressed against the uneven ground, stomach on the cool leaves underneath. A pine needle pressed against his side. He shifted slightly to get rid of the pressure.

260 yards, he thought. That was ...

The sight a little above the centre chest of the mortar gunner, he squeezed the trigger.

171

237.7 metres. This time he got the exact conversion right, but the thought was brushed away, unnoticed. Without waiting to see the effect of the bullet as it hit the man, he angled the barrel a fraction to the right, his hand already drawing the bolt back. The spent cartridge made a dull golden arc in the evening light, spinning out from the chamber on to the grass to his right. He hammered the bolt forward, the sight long fixed, once more, above the centre chest of the other man in the nest and fired again.

Artillery fire was growing again in the twilight, an almost continuous, booming barrage.

Good.

He angled the barrel to the left, without removing his eye from the sights, because if he did, he would have to focus and re-focus, which would take time, which he didn't have.

The man in the left machine gun position had not stirred. He was sitting, back to the wall, looking up at the sky.

Don't look around.

He sighted at the base of the throat. It was the only clear part he could see. A smaller target this time, but nearly the same distance. It didn't matter. He fired again.

Before the blur as he shifted the barrel to the third position on the right, he saw the man flung back under the impact of the bullet, sliding down and disappearing into the nest.

Another hit, his mind recorded. Now the second Type 92 machine gun. But there were two in this one, and it was dug deeper than the other two ...

Superior Private Isoya was thinking of home. It was a small islet off Honshu, almost an atoll. It was green, too, but crowded and noisy. It is crowded and noisy here as well, he reminded himself. The hills, the mist. Another bank of white wool was heading towards him, already covering one end of the hillside. There was no end to the mist. The rations had been good the past few days, he thought. Better than in a long time, ever since they reached this town. Perhaps supplies were improving?

His officers never told him anything. They made plans and they had ideas, but they never bothered to explain to him. The British were getting stronger than ever, he knew. At least the Colonel had posted him on this side, where all he had to do was wait for the odd unit from headquarters or watch the sky and the mist and listen to the gunfire.

'Will we get more supplies soon?' Private Noda, his gunner, asked.

'Maybe. Many things could happen. I am sure they will send more supplies from Burma.' Never say *I don't know* to your subordinates.

The Private subsided, stretching his legs in the cramped nest, hands on the 92, leaning back. Isoya resumed his position, legs crossed, looking at the sky. It would be evening ...

He felt the sudden blast of wind on his face. He heard a sound like a bowlful of thick sticky rice upset on a table near him: a solid liquid thump. He felt something warm spray in droplets on his neck. He *smelt* ...

He turned his head and watched, shocked, as Noda, neck almost torn in two by the force of the full-metal jacket Spitzer bullet, leaned slowly forward and came to a rest, head almost touching his ankles.

Where? What?! Someone was firing at them. The British were here! He crouched in the nest, slid the lever on the gun and fired a long burst, not lifting his head.

The boy saw the flashes in the waning light. The artillery fire was too deafening to allow the noise to be audible. The last man was firing at his hill, but in a different direction, nearer the Japanese positions to the north. He still hadn't been seen. Maybe they didn't think anyone would be firing from this distance.

Isoya stopped firing, lifting his head just barely to take a quick look. Where were they? He hadn't seen anyone on the road or the slopes. Where did they come from? The other machine gun and mortar should have opened fire by now. Why was no one else firing? He looked at the mortar nest. He couldn't see Arisue and Nishihara. Where had they gone, the idiots? They never left their posts.

He looked at the dead Private sharing his pit and a rapid realisation hit him. Were they dead, too? Where were the British soldiers?

He had to think quickly.

Now you are thinking, the boy said, trying to get into the Japanese soldier's head. You have realised by now the other men are dead. The radio is in the mortar nest. That is a hundred yards to your right. If you reach it, you can call for help and hide. Or you can wait in your trench for fifteen minutes for the soldiers to return. But you don't know how many of the enemy are there, or whether they are moving up to your position. Or you can show yourself now and make it easy for me. What will you do, Japanese?

The mist inched closer along the face of the other hill and over Imphal Road, muffling the big guns. The mist is closer, the evening is closer, the boy thought. There is not much time. Here is something to help you decide, Japanese …

Isoya crouched lower as bullets pinged against the tripod stalk of the 92, visible over the lip of the nest.

Just two shots. A sniper of some kind, or they don't want to fire all at once so I will think there aren't many? I could try running back up the hill, Isoya told himself. Once

I make it to the top and down the other side, I am safe. Or I can run to the radio.

He could try running to the hilltop, the boy reasoned, estimating the climb to the top from the nest. Two hundred yards, maybe a little less, but it was thick with pines. The man would be safe running among them until he emerged in a small clearing halfway up. The next time he would be visible would be at the top, outlined against the sky. But would he be fast enough? Was he a runner too?

Isoya looked back at the slope. It was safe, but he might not make it. He would slip on the muddy slope, grasping for creepers or pushing against tree trunks. He would be seen. The mortar nest was closer but in the open.

Run up the hill, Japanese. I will get you at the clearing, the boy thought, but didn't aim the rifle. Make it easy for me. Run up the hill and give me two chances.

I have to think like the British are thinking. What do they expect? They expect me to take the cover of the trees, Isoya thought ...

He scrambled up out of the trench, back first, nearly stumbled but *ran*, ran to the mortar nest, his body bent forward at an angle, his toes digging into the mud. Seventy-five yards, fifty yards, twenty, he was almost there, he had fooled the British ...

And the boy, his rifle sighted on the trail between the machine gun and the mortar, fired.

The bullet caught the Japanese at the base of the left ribs, travelling upward through the centre of the chest and exiting through the right shoulder, blowing the right collar bone to small pieces. Isoya was flung off his feet by the impact, crashing into the mud, head coming to a rest inches from the mortar trench.

Out-think whatever it is you are hunting, thought the

175

boy, remembering the old lessons, ejecting the round and chambering a fresh one, just in case.

He stood up, not bothering to clear the leaves and mud from his body and walked under the trees to the edge of the hillside. The mist was almost near his hide now, but he could still see down to the base of his hill. He held the rifle up in both hands. How had it become so heavy, he wondered. He held it up and waved, his body almost swaying with the load.

Far beneath him, men were running out of the trees across the cleared bank of the road, across the road, to the base of the other hill and into the mist.

He looked at the rifle, the stock nicked in places, the barrel striped with mud. He would clean it up nicely afterwards, he thought. It would look good once more.

That was done well. You didn't make a mistake at all.

Now he could sit and wait on the slope, hidden, for the men to return. He had cleared the first hurdle for them. They would find Mori. He did not need to be present for the execution and Meren would never allow him to get close to the Japanese, anyway. The rifle was getting very heavy. He placed it on the ground, took out his knife, looking at the hill opposite.

But, he had to *know*.

It was only a vertical slope downwards, a run across the road and a climb up a gentler slope.

This he had done before.

He gripped the knife and raced down the hill.

*

Mist again. This place was never free of it, thought the Colonel. He could see the positions through the trees from here. The British were firing again from Dog Hill. He could hear the howitzers too.

'Tell *Inu* to look out for attacks now,' he repeated to the radio operator. 'Their infantry likes to launch assaults in the evening.' The operator was bent over the radio, receiving and sending instructions.

'Tell the positions west of *Inu* to fire. I can see the howitzer positions,' Mori said needlessly. Everyone could see the howitzers where the British had gained ground on Garrison Hill.

But the Japanese guns in that sector were firing short, again.

He had sent another message to headquarters, telling them to rush more supplies of guns and ammunition. He had almost forgotten to add food to the list, but his aide had remembered. Send that too.

Headquarters had listened. It always listened to him. It had listened to his report and assurance that Kohima would be held and the British pushed back. It was only a matter of time. Meanwhile, he would override those pessimists at field headquarters, Sato and Miyazaki and the so-called soldiers. What did they know about tactics?

He imagined lines of men in green. Rows and rows of them. Columns upon columns of infantry. Towed guns, mortars, heavy machine guns, stacks of shells. The men, marching over the hills, firing from the trenches, occupying the positions of these stubborn defenders. The men yelling defiantly at the bombing aircraft of the British. Who needed the Air Force? War had always been fought on land, over land, by occupying armies, by infantry and cavalry and armour and big guns. They would march down to the plains, chasing the British lines before them. Many would fall, but he would have many more to replace them. Everyone would know his name: a conqueror, a commander. He would be remembered by Japan's history. More soldiers. More guns. More ammunition. We will get everything we ask for. We will push forward, and then ...

His aide was at his side.

'Colonel-*san*.'

He turned around. The aide, a shorter man, was looking up at him. He had said something but the Colonel had not heard.

'What is it?'

'In the compound.'

'What?'

The aide gestured silently with his hand, towards the door.

The Colonel listened.

'There is firing in the compound, Colonel-*san*.'

They both heard the gunfire and the shouts.

*

He ran uphill, pulling himself up with the creepers, pushing at the rocky face, the mud slippery under the ribbed soles of his tennis shoes, now layered with dirt and leaves. It was a lot more difficult running uphill after lying down in one spot for such a long time. He was beginning to feel a little wary, carrying a knife up to a hill with many guns and angry men. He should have kept a Sten too, but Imnuk might not have given him one, guessing his mind. In either case, it would be over before he reached ...

Much above him, the men had advanced in a wide line nearly to the top. Here they discovered, as the Angami had told them, the hilltop flattened and dipped into a broad cup screened from every side by the pines. In this cup they found the Japanese.

A group of them was getting ready to head downhill to the ledge to give company to the mortar and machine gunners for the night. There were two other trenches covered and camouflaged from the top and a few dozen soldiers on the ground.

Meren and half the men spread into a line to one side, the Angami and Imnuk took the other half around the pines, completely a circle that nearly reached the other end of the hilltop. Here the ground rose up in a final curve before dropping steeply down the vertical western face of the hill. A valley sparrow chirruped and before the Japanese noticed or commented that a bird had returned to Kohima by mistake, the raiders started firing from behind the trees.

The first few bursts caught the group readying to leave, in the open, the Stens hosing them rapidly. From the trenches the Japanese returned fire, but they had hardly any targets and were covered from all sides.

The boy heard the firing begin, pushed harder at the slope, nearly twisting his leg over a fallen branch. He crossed the ledge but didn't look at the trenches there, kept on running upwards, hearing a grenade explode ahead. The gunfire had decreased. At the hilltop, behind a tree, he saw two Nagas pause, throw down their guns, pull their *nok*s out and run silently over the rise, disappearing on the other side. No great battle cries while hunting.

He picked up one of the guns, found the magazine empty, threw it to one side and followed them.

He ran over the rise and into the cup, crashing into a Japanese soldier who had dropped his rifle or his courage and was trying to escape. The boy saw him rushing towards himself, remembered to pull back the knife and hold it with the elbow bent inward, the blade facing out as Imnuk had told him when dealing with boar, and hit the Japanese with

179

the full weight of his body, the knife going through the ribs. They fell together under the impact (the man was so *thin*), but the boy recovered on time, stood up without bothering to check and ran on around the rim of the cup.

The firing had stopped, the men had all brought their *nok*s out, the trenches were almost empty and the Japanese were everywhere, firing wildly or rushing with bayonets. The Konyak was fighting like a man possessed, his axe-like *nok* making large scything sweeps at three or four of the enemy. The boy recognised Subong, who had been at the house, swinging his *nok* at a Japanese. He couldn't see Meren or Imnuk anywhere, but then, everyone was looking different at the moment, fighting in the gunsmoke and mist.

From the corner of his eye he saw another Japanese rushing towards him with a bayonet. Gojen threw the knife, hitting him on the shoulder, making him drop the bayonet. Then the Japanese was on him, pinning him to the ground, hands around his throat. The boy made a fist and punched him at the throat, then a second time, but the man's eyes were wide and round with rage or fear, and he was strong. The boy got his right knee under him and pushed. The man loosened his grip but tightened it a moment later. The boy punched his throat again, harder. The grip loosened once more but stayed.

Someone picked up the Japanese from atop the boy and flung him away. Someone else finished the job with his *nok*. The Konyak pulled the panting boy up. If he recognised the boy, he gave no hint of it. He was bleeding from a couple of wounds. He looked like he had been shot. He hurried away to find more Japanese.

The boy looked around, found the knife he had dropped in the scuffle and ran towards the door he had seen, built into the rise at the far end of the cup. Somebody had thrown a grenade at it. The door stood on one hinge, half-open. Men were entering it.

And a Japanese poked his hand out from a trench and shot the boy with a pistol.

He felt a cold tingle on his left arm for less than a moment, and then red-hot pain erupted from his elbow to his bicep, the pain so biting he nearly lost his feet.

It was a poor shot with a handgun, one-handed and hurried. The bullet caught the boy on his left arm, cutting out a furrow upwards and exiting. Someone jumped into the trench before the Japanese could fire again.

Gojen dropped his knife, held his arm with his right hand and tried not to make a sound. He thought he was bleeding far more than the wound appeared.

He walked up to the door and stepped across it to the other side.

16

The gunfire and shouts followed too rapidly after each other. The shouts were in Japanese. Mori thought for a moment that the British had attacked down the road from the east. But they would not know to attack this post, would they? And his first line would have sent word …

A horrible thought struck him. What if Sato had lost his mind and decided to recover command of the invasion force by assassinating him? That would explain his men downhill not radioing back to him, wouldn't it? Sato had taken half his men with him the previous day and tried to take his mortar gun. It was all a conspiracy.

His head a mash of these thoughts, he took two doubtful steps towards the door and flinched at the sound of the grenade explosions, two of them, somewhere outside. More firing, more shouts. His aide was at the door, about to open it, hesitant.

The explosion knocked the Colonel off his feet, the bang nearly blowing in his eardrums. He was struggling to get back up when men rushed in. Angry men with wild eyes, in shorts—one of them bare-chested with fearsome tattoos all over him—carrying sub-machine guns. Another, who looked older than the rest, fired at the Major who had been wounded in the grenade explosion which had blown out the door, then turned the gun at the radio operator who was trying to rise from the stone slab on which he sat, drawing at his sidearm.

The Sten's burst caught the radio man across his waist and he fell to the floor, his earphones coming free and dangling from the radio. The bare-chested hillman turned his Sten on the radio, a long burst which brought its entrails—copper wire and filaments and things—out in a shower of metal.

They pulled Mori up on his feet and hit him. Then they hit him again, on the face. Something hard struck him in his stomach, knocking his breath out. He bent forward with the pain which seemed to go right through the stomach to his back. The leader had punched him. The 'combat' went out of the Japanese who had, all through his career, looked down on combat soldiers.

They pulled him by the hair, forcing him to look upwards. Their leader had a photograph in his hands. They looked at him carefully and at the photograph. Someone said, 'Mori?' and he turned his head automatically. They hit him a few more times.

He sagged down on his cot at one side of the room, but the men held him up roughly. The older man took out a long, wickedly sharp knife.

Someone else walked into the room, Mori saw. This one was bleeding from the left arm. He was a little shorter than the rest and looked much younger and, somehow, different. But he had the same look in his eyes.

The leader was shouting at the newcomer angrily, the Colonel heard, some hillman words. The other one was shaking his head and saying something. What were these savages doing here? Who were they to come and upset his world like this?

He looks a little different from the photograph, the boy

thought. A little older, a little thinner. But it was the same man. He went closer and looked at the Colonel: his face, his eyes, his uniform.

'Understand English?' Gojen asked, slowly. He should, shouldn't he, a senior army officer and all?

Certainly the Colonel knew some English: he liked interrogating English prisoners. He caught the savage's question, but the accent was different. He didn't reply.

'Understand?' asked the boy again, hands gesturing: 'One month ago'—one finger pointing behind—'village'—how do you signify a village?—'your soldiers, firing'—he pointed his right hand, mimicking a gun. 'Machine gun *g-r-r-r-r*,' he said, feeling almost foolish. 'People killed. Remember?'

What was he making those noises for, the little monkey? Mori thought. Is he telling me something? My soldiers did what, fired on people? *His* people? Is that what he is saying?

The boy gripped the collar of Mori's high-neck tunic and pulled it, hard, towards himself. 'One boy. There. Your ... men ... bayonet ... kill. Remember?'

What was he saying? This is so ridiculous, Mori thought.

'One ... boy,' pointing at himself, making little cutting motions. 'Kill. Remember. *Were you there?*' The last question was shouted at his face.

Mori cowered at the sudden outburst. What was he pointing at himself for? What incident? Killed who? There was just ... the boy with a knife ... *that one?* He remembered now.

The boy saw it in his eyes, the recognition. *You were there. You were giving orders.*

They came for the village? The wild half-animal his soldiers had caught?

The boy searched the Japanese face, looking for answers

184

to questions in a world he had no idea about just a few weeks ago. But there were no solutions here, no explanations for why men did such things.

The boy wanted to *do* things to him. He wanted to *hurt* this man, do anything which would make him feel better. But that was not the answer either, was it. It would not solve anything. It would not change anything.

It is easy to kill someone, he thought. It is perhaps even easier to order it. But to take away something which means a lot, an enormous lot to this man …

He searched his memory for Kenneally's background data on the Japanese. He liked being an officer, it said. He enjoyed the feeling of power.

He took a good grip on the man's collar—on which three white stars were fixed over a red-and-yellow striped field—and pulled hard. The stitching was of poor quality: the collar tore off easily.

Holding the piece of cloth in his hand, he looked at Mori, trying to tell him that he had taken something precious from him. Gojen tried to recall the British Army phrase when they court-martialled officers. He couldn't remember it at the moment: something about 'drumming you out'. He gave up. What was the use?

And Mori's carefully constructed fiction about the world and his place in it came apart just as rapidly as he realised what would happen. These strong, proud and angry men were yet more in the long line of bullies who had hounded him all his life and were here to end it for some petty reason. It was not fair.

He went tumbling down and down, deep into the great well of self-pity he had carried within himself all his life. His brilliant brother, his classmates at school, those bullies who had laughed at him all along, the brilliant officers he had served with and whom he had tried to outwit at every turn, all his inadequacies which he had directed at people wherever he went, his unhappy childhood, but he had tried, hadn't he, he had tried, he would have been better but …

'You used to beat me when I was young,' he said, not realising that his collapsing mind was saying the words aloud.

But in the eyes of the men around him, he saw no understanding, no pity. He saw nothing, as if they were saying: no one can blame his childhood for what he becomes. It is his choice and his alone.

The Colonel's knife was on a corner of the slab on which the destroyed radio stood. The boy took it, pointed it once in the direction of the cowering Japanese and walked out.

He found his throwing knife in the mud near where he had fought the second soldier. He looked around. The men were picking up their guns and whatever spent shells they could find, trying not to leave signs to identify who had been here. Some of the wounded were being bandaged. Subong was there. He caught the boy looking and smiled once, briefly. The rush had long since left the boy. He was feeling very tired and drained. His left arm was throbbing again.

Yajanlem, one of the Aos who had been at the council at KC's house, was dead in a trench. So was another Ao he recognised, and two others. The Konyak was dead too. He had been shot many times: the silent man had carried his grief with him to wherever people went afterwards, and perhaps had found his family again, if such things happened. The boy thought the Konyak had come here meaning not to return.

Imnuk came out, followed by Meren, their Angami host

186

and the others. It was time to leave. They would return north along the same route. The hunter clapped the boy on his shoulder, making sure it was not the left one.

'How does it look? Let me see.'

The bleeding was less now. The wound would leave a scar, but it was otherwise not a problem.

'Gojen …' said Imnuk, looking around at the hilltop.

'Hmm?'

'What was the man saying, at the end? He said something. It seemed he was trying to say something important.'

The boy considered it.

'I don't speak Japanese, Imnuk,' he said, shrugging his shoulders. *It doesn't matter*, he didn't say. Imnuk flinched a little when he heard the tone.

*

At 21.30 hours, that is, 9.30 p.m., Lt Gen. Sato met with his fellow officers. The counter-attack was due in half an hour. There was only a little problem.

'General-*san*, we can't raise *Saru*,' his radio officer said.

'Try again.'

But there was no signal from the observation post.

'When was the last communication?'

'At about 17.00 hrs, General-*san*.'

'There have been no messages since then?'

'No messages.'

They tried a few more times, but the post had vanished from the radio waves.

Sato made the obvious conclusion.

'Gentlemen, it seems we are under attack from the British from the direction of Imphal Road. They have overrun Mori's post and might even now be encircling *Saru*

Hill. He has either been captured or killed.'

His first thought, naturally, was whether other positions were under attack as well. This was what came from leaving the eyes and ears of the campaign with an officer like Mori: the campaign had been blinded at a stroke. But there had never been a choice.

He felt a huge relief at being rid of that madman, though from what he knew of him, Mori would have surely broken at the first sign of fighting and would probably spend the rest of his days in a British prison. It was better than he deserved. But this was not the time to talk about it. Sato had recovered control over his forces, at last. He had to consider the lives of his soldiers on the front line. It was not a difficult choice for him. He knew where his first duty lay.

'In such a situation, I will not risk the lives of our men in that area in an attack which might already be doomed. Order the attack force to withdraw, for the time being. We will consider the change in the situation and decide if we should attack later, after finding the exact positions of the British. And send word to 15th Army headquarters explaining it.'

He hoped his senior officers would understand and send help. The invasion was otherwise surely heading for failure. Why had he allowed his command to be hijacked by Mori?

The Japanese attack forces were stood down.

The British counter-attack went in at midnight.

17

'What do you make of it?' asked the Major of Intelligence the following evening.

He stood with Kenneally on the hilltop, looking around at the destruction: the trenches, the bunker built into the rising ground at one end. The bunker had a cot and stone slabs propped with logs for tables, crates of provisions. A long hole had been cut through the earth at the western end of the bunker. Through it they could see the hills spread beneath them. It was a great place for an observation post.

It was also the scene of what must have been a furious fight.

'It is certainly Mori,' Kenneally said. He was having mixed feelings at the moment. He had found his man, but it was a little too late.

Six hours of heavy fighting through the night into dawn on 24 March had driven the Japanese south from the base of this hill, but they still controlled Imphal Road and the hill positions to the south. The battle for Kohima was far from over, but for the first time, the counter-attack had given the British the initiative.

'What on earth happened here, sir?'

The first British forces on this hill had reported back that the scene did not make sense: a Japanese observation post, deep inside a Japanese-held area, wiped out in what seemed to be close-quarter fighting and not stray artillery fire. Kenneally, on being ordered to look into the matter, had kept his opinions to himself until he was certain about the identity of the man inside the bunker. That led to one possibility.

Sato had finally been pushed beyond the limits of his endurance and assassinated the Colonel. Kenneally could not blame the Japanese General: Mori must have been as much an embarrassment to the genuine Japanese officer corps as he had been just another criminal in uniform for British Intelligence.

What did not make sense was: why was *everyone* killed? Kenneally tried to re-imagine the scene, tried to picture the dusk, Japanese soldiers creeping up their own hill. Mori's men on the hilltop would have recognised them; some of them might even have been friends. It was unlike Sato to order the killing of his men. Why kill them all?

Something glinted in the mud nearby. He went and took a closer look.

'Did you find something, sir?' asked the Major.

Kenneally stood up from where he was kneeling. 'No. Nothing here.' He had to take a look at the three gun nests downhill.

These three, he thought, standing on the ledge near the mortar pit, these three should explain it. The mortar had been removed by the British to add to their shelling to the south, which was continuing at the moment.

Let's see. The gun crews can see up and down this road, so they can spot their people coming up. There had been a radio here, probably to communicate with Mori. Friendly forces or not, the men here would have been ordered by Mori to report *any* movement to him, paranoid as he was.

So, no. Whoever came up—and they would have to be a small number moving quicker than normal infantrymen—had to neutralise them first. But how?

He looked around, noted how close the eastern ridgeline came to the hill. The dense trees over there could be a good hiding place. The distance would be … far, but not far, if you put a marksman there. Someone good and well-trained. Somebody who could get all three nests without raising the alarm. A lot of planning would have gone into this. It could be possible.

'Major, we are certain there was no British unit operating here?'

'Definite, sir. It looks like one of our special operations' jobs, but there is only LRP, and it is in Burma.' The Long Range Penetration unit, or LRP, was a group of British special forces behind enemy lines in Burma, who had done just such small-scale search-and-destroy operations in the past.

'Hmm. No, certainly not them, or General Merill's Marauders either. It appears like a Stirling operation, doesn't it?'

A British officer, David Stirling, had started a special forces unit in northern Africa in 1941. His men had also done a good job in Egypt and elsewhere in the desert against the Germans and Italians. In fact, this new unit, named L Detachment, Special Air Service Brigade, by Stirling, was acquiring quite a reputation.

'In a way, sir. What do we do?'

But Kenneally was thinking of a conversation some time earlier with a soldier-turned-priest, a photograph he had passed on, some information. His first real confirmation that Mori was in India. *Somebody had died, but Bartlett hadn't given details. I hadn't asked.*

He was thinking of the stab wounds and cuts on some of the Japanese men he had found here. He was thinking of the spent cartridge he had picked out of the mud and was holding in his hand. The headstamp on the steel circle at its base read GBF. Greenwood and Batley Ltd, Farnham. A spent shell from a new British Lee-Enfield.

He was also thinking of a day in the trenches at the Somme in 1916, when the letter arrived telling him how his family had died. He was eighteen but had already learnt how hard the world was, and why family mattered. He was thinking of the way he had felt then, what he had wanted to do to those responsible, to men like Mori.

Somebody had decided to do something, finally, about such men.

But this also meant that the natives had new rifles. They were arming themselves, conspiring and acting on their own. They were acting outside the law he believed in. British law. This could become a problem for the government later, couldn't it?

He had his duty to do. Uncle Bill wanted a report. Uncle Bill would get a report.

*

They were inside Ao lands once more, sitting on the spur of a hill, facing the setting sun. The boy's arm was bandaged, but it throbbed now and then and he felt a large itch building up around the cotton wrap. Imnuk was sitting next to him, examining the knife they were bringing back. The Angamis had left them a short distance north of Kohima and returned to the town, back to the fighting.

Along the march back, it seemed that Meren wanted to take the boy aside and talk to him, but kept changing his mind.

'It is very nice to look at. How could a man like that have such a nice thing?' Imnuk was asking himself. And in truth, it was a beautiful knife or sword or whatever it was: the hilt and hilt-guard decorated with designs and animals. Japanese symbols ran up the blade almost to its tip.

The boy shrugged. It wasn't a matter he wanted to think about.

He still had a headache and pain in his ears from all that artillery and gunfire. In his satchel he had found the three Dum-Dums he had brought but never used. He held them in his hand. He flung them over the side and they went sailing down, far below.

'You could have kept them.'

'Fuller has many more of these. I can steal them any time.' But he didn't see any particular use for those bullets.

The sun went down in orange flames. A wind came up from the north.

The boy was thinking of what was to come after. There would be school, and more school. There would be more vacations at the estate, more things to learn. He wondered if his life at school and home would change now. He wondered if anyone he knew would understand if he even began to talk about all this. But who would he talk to? The stories never mentioned the real events, or what actually happened to the people inside them: what those people really thought, what they felt, what the story did to them.

There was a lot of pain in the world, but there was a lot of good as well. He would have to learn to value all the good things in his life, while assuming they would not last for ever. He would have to fix a set of lines and rules for dealing with the world. Some rules would work. *But*, as the lesson went, *not always*. He would have to learn.

The other matter was if the British ever found out about them, but Meren had explained the chances were really too small. After all, how would the British know that the Aos wanted Mori? No one in the hills would talk, that was certain.

But no matter what happened, his life would not be the same. A large part of it, the best part so far, had been taken away and would not be returned. The past seemed a long way off, and a haze was already beginning to fall on things he had thought would remain for ever.

The wind seemed to be carrying a lot of dust from somewhere, because he closed his eyes tight shut and was far away.

'*Oi*. What are you thinking about?'

'Nothing, Imnuk. I just remembered a story someone told us … me, long ago.'

Imnuk asked something but didn't get a reply. The hunter wanted to put his hand around the boy and say something comforting, but when he pulled Gojen around to face him, the boy had opened his eyes. Imnuk could see nothing in them, nothing at all, except a ferocious determination lurking just around the corner. The hunter changed his mind about comforting the boy, and they sat side by side, just two friends, waiting for the dusk.

18

'Do you want to hear the story of the End of the World?' asked Uti's mother to the two eight-year-olds, at Uti's home in Mokokchung, one afternoon. She was at the loom, weaving.

'The story of Molomi? Yes! Oi, *hati, xun,*' Uti poked his brother. Listen. No matter how many times she tells us. We like stories.

'Once, long ago, there came about the End of the World. To the hills of the Ao there came a great Fire from the East,' said the mother, her eyes round, her hands spread and gesturing, her voice deep and slow. 'The fire destroyed everything it touched, it went over and into every hill and ravine and valley, burning everything, leaving behind scorched, barren land. All the people and animals and birds ran here and there, trying to hide from the Fire. But the Fire was everywhere.

'Then, from the West, from the bank of the big River, there came a great wave of Water …'

'She means the Luit, Owl-nose.'

'Shh!!'

'The Water washed over the hills of the Ao, and it fought the Fire over hill and valley and ravine. The Fire was strong and terrible to see and it fought hard. But the Water was strong too and wouldn't give up. And up and down they fought for many terrible days, until the Fire turned around and ran over a hill and hid.

'The Water looked everywhere for the Fire, but it could not be found, it wanted not to be found. It was cunning. All the people and the animals and the birds said they did not know where it had gone. But the Grasshopper, with his eyes, saw everything.

'The Grasshopper is a clever little hunter …'

'Even better than the Mantis?' one or either of the boys would ask, each time. They knew the mantis very well and were afraid a little of the insect.

'Much better than the Mantis, his cousin. For the Mantis looks sinister, with his hands raised and folded, waiting for his prey. But the Grasshopper lies down in the leaves and grass and watches and no one is afraid of him.

'He had lain quiet and still, as only he can and he had seen where the Fire hid: inside bamboo and stone. And the Water went there and the Fire fled and the world became green again.

'And so, even today, if you rub bamboo and stone you can find small bits of the Fire hiding inside them. And the Grasshopper is still the most quiet and the most still, and he sees everything.'

Later …

'I wonder if it really happened,' Uti would say.

'Of course not.'

'You can't say that.'

'These things don't happen.'

'Maybe it did.'

'Then maybe we don't know the whole story. Maybe there was a reason the Grasshopper didn't run and hide, like everyone else.'

'You don't know anything, *Hati*!'

'Owl-nose!'

196

EPILOGUE

IC-6E/G641

To,
Imperial General Staff
Forward Field HQ
14th Army HMAS   25 April 1944

REPORT OF INVESTIGATION

As directed by CO 14th Army Lt Gen. Slim, I have inquired into the events on the night of 23 April on Kuki Picquet, behind then positions of the Imperial Japanese Army. I present the findings as under:

The hill (referred by the IJA as Saru Hill) was defended on the night of the events by their positions at the base of the western face. The eastern face, approachable by a narrow slope, contained three IJA gun nests (of which our forces were not aware during the occurrence of the events). The top of the hill appears to have contained a camouflaged forward observation post under 1st Communications Unit, 31st Division of the IJA. Questioning of captured prisoners from 31st Division IJA has confirmed that the post was commanded by **Colonel Shunroku Mori**, lately attached with 15th Army IJA.

Interrogation of prisoners captured in our counter-attack of 24 April has indicated that **at or between 1700 and 2400 hrs April 23**, this camouflaged post was attacked by unidentified men of unspecified number who appear to have come along

197

Imphal Road. (Note: This road and its southern approaches continue to be held by Japanese forces.) The three gun positions which guarded the approach uphill were neutralised and the remaining forces on the hilltop were also neutralised, evidence indicates.

Colonel Mori was found dead inside his communications room when our divisions overran the hill later on 24 April. His identity has been personally confirmed by me.

I have satisfied myself that no Allied unit, infantry or special forces, was operating behind Japanese lines at this period in this area. Looking at the amount of force used in the assault and the evidently complete element of surprise, it can be concluded that 31st Division CO Lt Gen. Sato and other senior officers, who were known to have severely unfriendly relations with Colonel Mori, had directed this operation in order to assassinate him, and units familiar to soldiers guarding the post were used. No other explanation appears to suffice.

As our records show, Colonel Mori was suspected to have been behind mass civilian killings in China, Singapore and Burma and therefore the IJA might not be willing to take up the matter at a later date. There is insufficient evidence to prove this conspiracy, which, it may be pointed out, becomes an internal matter of the IJA, with no connection to us.

However, in the event the matter of his death is raised by IJA 31st Division staff, and the hand of British forces is alleged to cover the suspected role of Japanese officers, HM Intelligence Corps advises complete denial of involvement or any knowledge about these events.

Sd/
J. Kenneally
Lt Col., HMIC

The report was duly filed and squirrelled away inside the records of the 14th Army. History does not say if General Slim got around to reviewing it afterwards, or if he even referred to the events any time later in his illustrious career.

But we *do* know that, at that point, he was getting ready for what would turn into the longest campaign of the Second World War. Beginning with the siege of Kohima and ending when Japanese forces in Burma surrendered in spring 1945, the Burma Campaign would go down in history as the beginning of the retreat of Japanese forces in Asia. In the middle of such events, it is doubtful, if at all, General Slim considered the unusual incident on a small hilltop. But it can be supposed that he, an admirer of Baron Carl von Clausewitz's military theories, would have explained it as one of those strange things that happen within what that Prussian officer had called 'the fog of war'.

Acknowledgments

Historical fiction, like history, is a collaborative effort. This story would not have been written if it weren't for:

Chris Hunt of the Imperial War Museum, Kent, England, who pointed me in the right direction during my initial research on battle tactics in the Burma Campaign;

Rupam Jyoti, Navaneet, Mriganka, Manas and all the Boys back home who very enthusiastically egged me on during my travels in the North-east and Burma and who provided an op base in Guwahati;

My uncle Bimal and his lovely family at Digboi for the forward op base while I took a look at Assam and Burma's oil belt during the war;

All the officials and staff at the State Museum, Guwahati, for throwing open their collection and archives with a smile;

Peihau Nsarangbe, Research Assistant, Art and Culture at Kohima Museum for his guidance while I researched the Battle of Kohima and for his insight into the Ao Nagas;

U Phrien, policeman and poet, who dexterously guided me during my stay at Tamu, Burma and arranged for just the right rifle and bullet;

Colonel M.C. Baruah, Mahar Regiment, Gajraj Corps, for helping solve a particularly knotty ballistics issue and M.L., on the Other Side, for his views on the art and science of hunting man;

Mel Ewing and all the big guys at Sniper Central for their knowledge, encouragement and advice;

Everybody at Scholastic India, for everything, from the beginning to the end, which made telling this story such a pleasure, particularly Sayoni, who gently let me totter through several deadlines and Shantanu, who started it all by making me return to something I had left behind and

My late grandfather, to whom this story is dedicated.